SURPRISE REUNION IN CROATIA

ELLA HAYES

Harlequin

ROMANCE

Harlequin® ROMANCE

Recycling programs for this product may not exist in your area.

ISBN-13: 978-1-335-47094-2

Surprise Reunion in Croatia

Harlequin Enterprises ULC
22 Adelaide St. West, 41st Floor
Toronto, Ontario M5H 4E3, Canada
www.Harlequin.com

HarperCollins Publishers
Macken House, 39/40 Mayor Street Upper,
Dublin 1, D01 C9W8, Ireland
www.HarperCollins.com

Printed in U.S.A.

1 2 3 4 5 6 7 8 9 10 HDC 28 27 26 25

Passport to Paradise

Final destination: happily-ever-after!

The heat is rising, adventure is calling...
So why not strap in and get swept away to the
world's most luxurious locations? Lands of white sands,
blue skies—and sizzling nights...

Follow our intrepid travelers as they check their
baggage and lose themselves in first-class romance. But
are their connections just for the summer...or are these
jet-setters en route to their five-star forever afters?

Grab your ticket for...

Marriage Ruse in Paradise by Susan Meier

Hired for One Tuscan Summer by Jessica Gilmore

Faking It for the Cameras by Justine Lewis

Surprise Reunion in Croatia by Ella Hayes

One Bed Between Rivals by Joss Wood

Available now!

Her Big Fake Greek Wedding Date by Michele Renae

Coming next month!

Dear Reader,

Confession: There's a little bit of my own past in this story...

I once had a crush on a boy who played the drums. He looked just fine sitting behind that drum kit, biceps flexing as he hit those beats. Sigh! For a brief, tantalizing moment, I felt a glimmer of interest from his side, but then almost instantly it fizzled out. I got over the crushing disappointment, but the memory lingers, so perhaps it was inevitable that it would emerge in a fictionalized form one day.

Of course, my hero, rock star drummer Finn Falco, is markedly different from my own high school crush, aside from his sunny nature and nice arms, that is. I've given him a past secret crush on my heroine, jilted bride Izzy Valentine, who worshipped him back in the day but never got to show it. Now Izzy is honeymooning solo on Hvar, trying to make sense of her life, just as Finn is there with his band to record a new album.

One chance encounter later they are face-to-face again...

I hope you enjoy reading Izzy and Finn's *Surprise Reunion in Croatia* as much as I enjoyed creating it.

Love,

Ella x

After ten years as a television camerawoman,
Ella Hayes started her own photography business
so that she could work around the demands of
her young family. As an award-winning wedding
photographer, she's documented hundreds of
love stories in beautiful locations, both at home
and abroad. She lives in central Scotland with her
husband and two grown-up sons. She loves reading,
traveling with her camera, running and great coffee.

Books by Ella Hayes

Harlequin Romance

Her Brooding Scottish Heir
Italian Summer with the Single Dad
Unlocking the Tycoon's Heart
Tycoon's Unexpected Caribbean Fling
The Single Dad's Christmas Proposal
Their Surprise Safari Reunion
Barcelona Fling with a Secret Prince
One Night on the French Riviera
Bound by Their Lisbon Legacy
Driving Her Impossible Billionaire

Visit the Author Profile page at Harlequin.com.

This one is for all those who remember their own high school crush, and for all the hot drummers too!

CHAPTER ONE

Finn Falco lifted his glass and looked out over the archipelago.

What a sunset! Fiery red, blistering at its fringes into scattered shades of orange and pink and gunmetal grey. It demanded reverence, respect, absolute focus—but how to give it any of those things with all this distracting commotion going on?

The music on its own had been fine, just a throb in the background, but now there was clapping and cheering as well, getting louder, spilling out across the terrace from inside the bar.

Something was kicking off.

Crazy, the tug of it. Anyone would have thought he was a stranger to the sound of applause.

Geez! And imagine even having that thought, but it was somehow true. He was an old hand now, should have been able to absorb the clapping and cheering like blotting paper, make himself *not* be curious. He should have been able to sit tight, content himself with what he had got right here—spectacular sunset, nice cold one in his hand—but there it was.

No good!

He drained his glass and got up, heading for the bar entrance. He had to go look. It might be a talking dog or some other marvel worth seeing. And it wasn't as if there wouldn't be other sunsets. The way things were going with the band, this new album was going to take weeks to record—not that he was complaining.

He felt a rise in his chest. Definitely not complaining! Croatia was the bomb, Hvar island a joy. Myriad little turquoise coves to explore. Crystal-clear water to swim in. And fish that would come right up to your legs if you stood still for long enough. Okay, so maybe the tempting white beaches were gritty in reality, a tad hard on the feet, but they were easy on the eye, as were the Mediterranean pines and the olive trees, the vineyards and the quaint, pale, ancient buildings in the towns.

The best thing about being here, though, the icing on the cake, was *not* being recognised. Who knew how sweet that could feel after the insanity of the past year, how grateful he could feel that the band hadn't made it in Croatia yet? For sure, there were still late summer tourists about who might have twigged who he was if he'd had Jaxon and the others in tow, but he didn't. They had all gone back into the studio after dinner with their producer, Antonio Horvat, to argue some more about artistic direction and about how the new album should 'sound'.

Not his bag! Whatever the 'sound', beats were just beats at the end of the day.

Not true, of course, not what he really believed, but saying it got him off the hook with the others, kept him clear of the fray, and that was the main thing. Keeping clear of the clashing egos. The aggro. Because who needed that? Not him, not after growing up with three brothers and three sisters going at it hammer and tongs all the livelong day, Ma and Pa joining in for good measure. God help him, he loved them all to pieces, loved that he could help them out with money these days, but getting a word in edgeways at home had always felt like too much effort. Easier to smile and bow out, keep his thoughts to himself. And now it had become a habit to take the path of least resistance. Ingrained. As indelible as the ink on his arms.

But it was cool. Let the others thrash it out. Once they had got the 'sound' nailed, he would get himself behind his drum kit and smash it as always. Until then, it was downtime central. *Playtime!* Exploring the island on his motorcycle, swimming with the fish, blissfully indulging every daft whim that seized him, such as checking out what was going on inside that bar.

And now here was the entrance, exhaling its fug and noise. He re-tightened his hair tie, took a breath and stepped through.

Heaving. Muggy. Dim. But not dim enough to conceal the star attraction. Not a talking dog—*surprise, surprise!*—but a girl—*naturally!*—in a short, clingy, silver sequinned dress, dancing barefoot on a table, shaking her delectably curvy little rear at a rapt crowd of guys who were cheering her on.

Mesmerising!

He shifted stance. But also unsettling somehow. The spectacle of it…

Those guys.

He swallowed hard. How *not* to be like them, though? How *not* to watch her when she was so, seemed so…

Oh God! The *way* she was moving her body. So sinuous. So uninhibited. Smooth, pale legs, flexing muscles. Breasts rising into the loose cowl of her dress. And what about that slim waist? He could feel his hands yearning to go there, just to feel the fluid swaying motion of her body, her rhythm and beat, all of her lovely heat.

Snaking her fairy arms up over her bent head now, swinging her long, fair hair as she gyrated, lost in the music, in a world of her own somehow. Or maybe she was lost in a drunken haze—hard to tell from here—circling, turning round degree by tantalising degree. And then suddenly, as if she'd just come to, she brought her head up with a toss of her hair, and a spasm shot across his stomach and down to his toes.

Izzy!

He squeezed his eyes shut, shook himself, looked again, but it was still Izzy, up on *that* table, wearing *that* dress. Not a dress he could have imagined her wearing in a million years. Then again, it was about a million years since he last saw her, wasn't it? People grew up, changed. He had, so why not little Izzy Valentine?

Cripes... But this was some transformation. Could it really be her, Carl's shy twin sister? The girl who had opened up his eyes, rocked his world at that first school show rehearsal they'd done when they were sixteen? The girl he had never really noticed before that, because she and Carl never hung out, didn't share any friend groups, Carl joking that nine months in the womb with Izzy had been nine months too many! The girl who had been there on the stage, doing that Girls Amok song with two of her friends, hanging back a bit, somewhat reluctant, but hitting the notes, hitting the beats, shining brighter than the other two put together, brighter even than the sun. The girl he suddenly couldn't *stop* looking at, noticing, the girl he wanted to get to know, be with, hold, kiss. The one he would hide himself in the wings just to watch. And the one who had come hurrying off the stage that time and barrelled right into him so that he'd had to catch her arms to steady her. She had looked up into his eyes, and he had felt the floor tilting and his body tingling, and it had started to feel like a moment, as if something magical was happening between them. And he had wanted it to happen, from the depths of his ardent, infatuated soul, but then suddenly fear had crashed in, filling his head with thoughts...

Carl's sister! Are you mad? Carl! The one person who lets you get a word in edgeways, listens to you instead of talking over you. Your best friend, your bud, your bro! You can't jeopardize that, risk messing up things with him. Forget it, Finn, let it go!

So he had backed away, bolted for the exit, kept his eyes away from hers forever afterwards so she wouldn't think he liked her, wouldn't go and start making doe eyes at him in front of Carl and give him away.

He drew her back into focus. Now here she was on Hvar, cavorting on tables, and here he was again, watching her...

His heart paused.

Hang on, though...

Last time he'd spoken to Carl—over a year

ago because of all the band stuff and because Carl was married to the hospital—hadn't Carl said that Izzy had set a date for her wedding? Carl must have mentioned the date, but Finn was damned if he could remember it. Too drunk to lock it in, probably. Drunk because of Janine. And because, why lock it in? Just a wedding, *finally*, after the longest engagement in history!

He zoned in on her left hand. Gold thumb ring. No other rings.

His heart pulsed. Was that why she was up there acting like a wild child? Was this Izzy, celebrating her freedom?

He looked at her face. *No...* This wasn't a celebration. Oh, she was working it all right, partying hard, but there was an edge to her, something desperate going on. Mouth drawn tight. *That dress...* Fitting for a nightclub, but incongruous here. And those guys watching her... Flushed faces. Hungry, feverish eyes.

He felt a knot tightening inside him. This wouldn't end well. All this flaunting and teasing could only end up with her in the arms of one of those beer-soaked losers, and maybe that was what she wanted, but could he really stand by and watch it happen, watch—

God Almighty!

Grabby hands, reaching up now, trying to catch hold of hers, jolting the table.

No way!

He launched himself into the crowd, using his shoulders, his height, his stride, keeping his eyes locked on Izzy and on the guy.

The damned idiot was going to pull her off balance, pull her right off that table, hurting her, and he couldn't let that happen—*couldn't!*

He pushed harder, forcing his way through the endless jostle of bodies and then, at last, he was there, able to muscle himself between Izzy's table and the lumbering grabby-handed guy. He planted his feet wide to fill the space, make a buffer zone, and looked up into the hazy startled beam of Izzy's wide, most definitely inebriated gaze.

No time for pleasantries. No time for getting over the close-up shock of her drunken loveliness. The rescue was the thing. Only that.

He thrust his hand up, holding it out to her, making his tone urgent so she would wake up to the danger she was in. 'Izzy, for God's sake, come down from there before you fall!'

Finn Falco!

Here!

Seriously?

Izzy screwed her eyes shut to block him out, felt her hands curling into tight little balls.

No, no, no, no, no. This could *not* be happening. Not *this*! Wasn't it enough for fate that it had already dealt her the mother of all blows, saddling her with a fiancé who had decided at the literal eleventh hour to bail on her, *not* go through with the wedding that she had spent the last ten months meticulously planning? Wasn't it enough for fate that she was humiliated, bruised and broken—needing to let off some angry steam, needing to drink and dance and maybe take one of these nice Swedish lads back to that vast empty honeymoon bed for some hot, sweaty, no-strings sex, just for the hell of it, just to see how it would feel—without it dealing her this cruel, extra little twist?

Finn Falco! Of all people! The one who had stolen her heart back in high school with his amber eyes and tangly red-brown hair, the one who had beguiled her with his lovely face, and his lovely height, and his lovely shoulders. The one she had burned for right to her very tips, the one whose name she had scribbled inside endless hearts in her secret diary. The one who had played drums with his band in all the school shows, looking so hot in his T-shirt with his gorgeous honed arms. The one who had been the *only* reason she had let her friends talk her into doing the show too when she was sixteen. A silly Girls Amok number. All to see him, be around him, breathing the same air. The one she had longed to talk to. Get to know. The one she had desperately wanted to kiss...

And also the one who had given her that deep, yearning look in the wings that time, then run off, leaving her feeling *this* small, *this* inconsequential. The one who had ignored her forever afterwards, even though he was Carl's best friend and came to the house all the time. The one who had made her feel gauche and pointless, stupid and invisible. *Less* than invisible...

She forced her eyes to open. And now here he was, *somehow*, looking up at her, meeting her actual gaze with his actual gaze for only the second time in his whole damn life, reaching his hand up towards her, waiting for her to take it to... what? *Save* her?

What to make of it? Of him? Of his outstretched hand?

Putting the past aside, it was a noble gesture not lost on her, but neither was the faint look of disapproval in his eyes.

Some nerve!

Where did he get off, disapproving of *her* having a good time with these lovely guys when he was hardly a paragon of virtue himself? Up to his neck in girls at school, getting up to all sorts with them by all accounts, and now he was *still* up to his neck in women—every photograph a different story, a different woman. Not that she spent her time poring over his pictures or any-thing. It was just impossible *not* to see them everywhere these days—as impossible as it was to switch on the radio and *not* hear an 'Olive' track playing, Jaxon Cairns's deep, melodious—

'Hey!'

She blinked. Ruben…? Or was this one Henrich? Names, faces blurring. *Whatever!* He was rallying, squaring himself up after Finn's interruption.

'What's happening, Izzy?' He shot a red-rimmed glance in Finn's direction. 'Who's the party pooper?'

Where to even begin…?

'I'm a friend.' This from Finn, smiling pleasantly, shifting his shoulders slightly, a gesture that made him seem bigger somehow. 'And she's with me, okay?'

With him?

On what planet…?

'Is that true, Izzy?' Ruben-or-Henrich was looking at her again, his gaze suddenly wary. '*Are* you with him? Is he your damn boyfriend or something?'

She felt a hot wave pounding up her spine. Way to bring her teenage Finn fantasies thundering back up to the boil, make her cheeks flame the way they had used to whenever he was around. Just as well the pain was rising, too. Pain was armour—something she could use.

She shook her head, managing to scoff. 'No, I'm not with him.' And just in case Finn had a notion that she was lapping this up, enjoying this scrap of his sudden, inexplicable, undivided attention, then why not put him straight, launch one back, sting him the way he had stung her all those years ago?

She turned to look at him, raising her eyebrows. 'And he's one hundred percent definitely *not* my boyfriend.'

His gaze rippled, registering the slight, then cleared again. 'Izzy, please…' Shaking his head now, moving closer, still holding his hand out to hers. 'You're tipsy at best, and these lads are beyond drunk, can't you see?' He glanced at the Swede, and then his eyes came back, pleading. 'This guy… There'll be an accident if you don't get down.'

No discernible disapproval now. Only concern etched on his face. An older face, of course, lightly tanned, lightly bearded in the Viking style. *Even more handsome…* And his hair was still that gorgeous red-brown tangle, but it was long now, long enough that he had got it pulled back and up into a bun. Fine silver chain around his neck. Some sort of pendant just visible below the neckline of his grey marl T-shirt. Silver ring on his thumb. He looked the part, every inch the rock star drummer, with his broad shoulders and honed bicep muscles and thick forearms—inked from wrist to elbow. Almost a cliché, but he was to die for all the same, which she knew, because she had died that death a long time ago. And for that, she wanted to knock his hand away, give him his marching orders. But actually doing it…

She swallowed hard. *Too harsh!* And ungracious. Especially when he was right about everything. They *were* all drunk. Horribly so. Rakija shots lined up on the bar. *How many…?* But the guys had been downing beers as well, dropping in chaser bombs and suchlike. And then they had persuaded the barman to turn up the music, and the beat had felt like magic. And there had been no space on the floor to dance, so she had kicked off her shoes and got up onto the table. It had been the best feeling in the world, dancing out the bitterness and hurt in this glitzy, overpriced, completely inappropriate dress that Eddie's credit card was paying dearly for. Was he ever going to regret trying to assuage his guilt by giving her free licence with it! But Ruben-or-Henrich *had* been grabbing for her hand just now, knocking into the table, and she *had* almost lost her balance which was obviously what Finn had seen, why he was standing here right now, and why she herself did not have a leg to stand on. The grain of a thumping headache, yes, but a leg, no. And so…

She drew a breath. 'Okay, Finn, you win…'

A momentary relief played over his features

and then suddenly, in a single strong swift move-ment, she was being seized, lifted and lowered back to the floor. For a glorious, muddling sec-ond, his arms stayed tight around her and then they fell away, and he was stepping back, rak-ing a lock of hair behind his ear.

'Have you got some shoes?'

Not *So how have you been, Izzy?* or *Wow! Isn't this weird?* Then again, they didn't exactly have anything to fall back on, did they? No old con-versations to dip into, no shared experiences, except for that moment in the wings, and like hell was she bringing that up, the tingling hope of it, the crushing pain.

No. All they had were shoes. Shoes she would quite like to have back on her feet since with-out them, Finn was towering above her, making her feel even smaller and more pathetic than she felt already with her rakija breath, and her silly hot face, and her stupid sparkly straps slipping down her shoulders.

She nodded. 'Yes, they're around here some-where...' She tugged at her dress straps, scan-ning the floor beneath the table, but Finn was already there, crouching to the task.

'I see them...' He stretched, reaching, his T-shirt tautening across his back, leaving noth-ing to the imagination as far as his musculature went. Then he was springing back up, raising an eyebrow in her direction. 'Red soles?' He tidied the shoes together, then handed them over. 'Very nice.'

'Thanks.'

So he knew about Louboutins! She bent to put them back on, trying not to wince at the unfamiliar pinch. Then again, of course he would know. Those women he dated probably had cupboards full of designer shoes, unlike herself. She didn't care about stuff like that. She had only bought these to go with the dress—courtesy of Eddie's credit card, of course.

Vendetta dress.

Vendetta shoes.

Instruments of torture all round.

And on the subject of torture…what to do about Finn?

Yes, he had saved her from a likely fall, and yes, he had retrieved her shoes, but they weren't friends, so why pretend otherwise? There was no reason to prolong this encounter. He must have somewhere to go, plans of some sort, and she had Paradise Villa, didn't she? Not that spending a third sad and lonely honeymoon night in that remote, luxurious, godforsaken love nest was what she'd had in mind for tonight, but none of the Swedish guys was going to be interested in hooking up with her now. She bit back a sigh.

Her first ever no-strings fling would just have to wait until tomorrow. As for Finn…

She straightened, scooping up her clutch from the edge of the table, then raised her eyes to his. 'So… Thanks, I guess.'

His eyes crinkled. 'Any time, Izzy.'

Any time? *This*, after ignoring her for years, after never giving her even a single second of his time! *This*, complete with crinkly-eyed smiling and sustained, normal eye contact.

Quite the turnaround!

But she couldn't let herself get snagged on Finn's whys and wherefores. She had come to Hvar for herself—to hide, and to cry, to bounce herself off a few walls, to get Eddie out of her system—or try to, at least. She had come here to debrief, shake herself down. Rationalise. Accept. Heal. Find peace. Make a new life plan. All of the cathartic things. She had not come here for Finn Falco. He was not part of her equation and the sooner she could get herself out of here and away from him, the sooner she'd be able to forget this entire excruciating episode.

She steadied herself, returning his smile for the sake of politeness because he *was* Carl's friend, even if he wasn't hers.

'Thanks, but it won't be necessary.' She adjusted her grip on her bag, using the moment to calibrate her tone along the lines of firm and pleasant. 'I'm going to go now. Goodbye, Finn.'

'Okay…' His gaze flickered a little. 'Bye, Izzy.'

She turned herself one-eighty, setting her sights on the door.

Well, that had been easy enough! *Goodbye, Finn. Bye, Izzy.* All very civil, very grown-up.

Unlike getting herself wrecked on rakija shots!

Such dear little glasses. Such clear, innocent-looking liquid. So warming, but deadly on an empty stomach—Eddie's fault because getting anything solid past her lips had been impossible since…

She paused, considering the door. No closer for all the steps towards it she was taking. These people in the way weren't helping, and neither were these shoes.

Damned six-inch heels! *Who* in their right mind would ever wear six-inch heels? Rubbish for dancing in, and patently no good for walking in either. In fact, maybe the thing to do would be to take them—

'Hey.'

Finn! Somehow beside her again, looking down at her, a hint of a twinkle in his eyes.

'Can I be of help at all?'

Her chest tightened. He was being kind, perhaps, but also laughing at her behind his eyes for being useless, for making zero progress. Well, there was such a thing as pride, such a thing as clutching at the last shreds of one's dignity.

She lifted her chin. 'With what?'

'With getting you out of here.' He glanced round at the crowd, then shrugged his nice shoulders. 'It's hard to make any headway through this lot, especially in shoes like that, I should imagine…'

She bit down on her lip hard. Damn his sweet gallantry—citing the shoes and the crowd as impediments to her progress and not the quantity of alcohol in her bloodstream. Impossible not to warm to him just a little bit for that, and she didn't *want* to warm to him, didn't want to start sliding down that old slippery slope.

'Come on, Izzy, it's a no-brainer.' Dipping his chin at her now, smiling into her eyes. 'If you let me help you, you'll be out of here in no time.'

Maybe so, but that would mean saying goodbye to him all over again outside, wouldn't it? And it would never sound as good—as *final*—as she had made it sound before. On the other hand, since he was here now, in front of her, she was going to have to say goodbye to him again anyway, even if she *did* turn him down. *Unbelievable!* Yet again, he had left her without a leg to stand on and yet again, the only way forward was to concede.

She set her lips to stop a sigh coming out. 'Okay, Finn. You win.'

CHAPTER TWO

THAT PHRASE AGAIN—*you win*—as if this was a fight they were having.

Was Izzy one of those types who got feisty after a few drinks, taking on the world, taking no prisoners? *Whatever!* The hostile treatment was starting to wear thin. Couldn't she see he was simply trying to take care of her?

He searched her face, her eyes. Okay, so maybe not, given the state she was in. Benefit of the doubt and all that.

He freshened his smile, opening out his arm to her. 'Okay then, so if you just want to...'

Her gaze flared, then narrowed. 'You want to put your arm around me?'

He felt the arm in question dropping like a stone.

Who knew that little Izzy Valentine could be such a monumental pain in the tush? Maybe it was time to ditch the subtlety, call a spade a spade.

'It's not a question of *want*, Izzy! It might have

escaped your notice, since you're three sheets to the wind, but you're struggling to walk right now, which means the best way out of here, short of me actually picking you up and carrying you, is for you to cling on and let me steer you. If you have a problem with that and don't want my help, then fine. I'll bow out and leave you to it, tell Carl it's what you wanted.'

'No!' Her eyes flew wide. '*Please!* Don't say anything to Carl...' Biting her lip. 'I'm sorry, okay? I'm a mess. Beyond the pale. I know it. It's just that...' Her eyes flickered, then locked onto his, searching for who knew what. And then, as if she had drawn a blank, or just got tired, she let out a sigh. 'I'm not... This isn't... I don't—'

'I know.'

Which he didn't, logically, because he had never allowed himself to get to know her, had he? Yet for some reason, it felt true. What also felt true—*right*—was taking decisive action, seizing the moment.

'Come on...' He opened his arm again, not waiting for her this time but tucking her in tight—all the sticky, sparkly warmth of her— and making for the door, lifting her when he felt her feet stumble, not stopping until he had got her to a vacant table on the terrace, because asking her first would undoubtedly have landed him in another pointless debate, and what was *not* debatable was that Izzy needed some fresh air and a very large glass of water.

He pulled out a chair, guiding her into it, then sat himself down opposite, catching the eye of the young waitress who had served him his beer before. Two minutes later, the girl was setting down a large jug of water and two glasses, glancing at Izzy with poorly masked disdain.

His heart caught a little. No more disdain than Izzy was clearly feeling for herself at this moment. Downcast eyes, blushing cheeks, fingers twisting into her bag strap. Silence.

Maybe he shouldn't have mentioned Carl. But he was only human. Absorbing that barbed *'he's one hundred percent definitely* not *my boyfriend'* remark was one thing, but the snarky way she had said *'You want to put your arm around me?'* had really stung, since putting his arms around her was all he had ever wanted to do all those years ago. Well, maybe not *all* he had ever wanted to do, given his age and rampaging hormones but, *whatever*! She had put him on the defensive, so he had brought up Carl to knock her off her high horse, make her think that he was only helping her out of duty because she was Carl's sister.

Juvenile!

But there it was. Meanwhile, she needed water.

He poured a glass, offering it over. 'Here, you should drink this…'

Her fingers stopped their relentless twisting and took it, and then her eyes lifted, smudgy with make-up, full of catchlights from her dress and from the glowing bulbs strung above their heads.

'Thank you.' She took a few long, slow sips, looking round at the terrace, then her eyes came back, her gaze softer than before, apologetic. 'And seriously, thanks for getting me down off that table, and for finding my shoes, and for bringing me out here, and for this…' She sipped again, nodding, as if to herself. 'I *so* need to re-hydrate.'

He felt his heart softening, a smile trying to emerge. Now *here* was the Izzy he recognised, the Izzy he had used to watch covertly from behind his locker door, talking and laughing with her friends, her eyes shining. A woman now, obviously, not a girl, and not exactly laughing either, but Izzy just the same.

'You're welcome.' He filled his own glass. 'As it happens, I know a thing or two about rehydration. I've been where you are more than a few times myself.'

She made a little scoffing noise. 'I'm sure you have…' A wry light entered her gaze. 'I mean, isn't drinking de rigueur for famous rock stars, along with sex and drugs, et cetera?'

Teasing him, sort of, but teasing was fine. He could do teasing all day long.

He set the jug back down. 'Absolutely! You know, there's actually a rock star pledge they make you take—expected behaviour—although I had to draw a line at the whole hotel-room-trashing thing because Ma would have my guts for garters if I ever did anything like that.'

'But she's okay with the sex and the drugs?'

'No, not at all.'

Poor Ma. She would have been cuffing his ears if she knew he was raiding her larder for amusing material, but Izzy was on the hook now, and he wanted to keep her there because talking to her, seeing the light playing through her gaze, felt so damned good.

He pursed his lips, channelling his mother. 'Ma one hundred percent disapproves of sex.'

Frowning. 'But, like…haven't you got loads of brothers and sisters?'

His heart trilled. Could she have given him a better cue if she had tried?

He nodded. 'Yes, and see, I think that's the reason right there. As for drugs—and tattoos for that matter—she's dead against those as well.'

'And yet you went and got yourself a pair of sleeves!'

'A moment of rebellion, for which I'm paying dearly.'

She regarded him for a beat, and then a slow smile curved on her lips, making his heart sing. 'You're funny.'

'Thank you, unless you mean funny in the head, which might well be the case since—' he pointed downwards, whistling the long descending cartoon note that was his party trick '—I might well have been dropped on it as a baby.'

Turning her face away now, but the laughing dimple in her cheek was a dead giveaway. Beyond gratifying after all the feisty stuff. But then suddenly, the dimple was gone, and she was turning back again, propping her elbow on the table, resting her chin in her hand.

'So, changing the subject, have you spoken to Carl recently?'

His heart fell. Way to put a massive dent in things. How was he supposed to tell her he hadn't, just minutes after using Carl to score one back at her in the bar?

No getting around it, though. Carl was literally the only thing they had in common, ergo, he was the next most obvious topic of conversation. Nothing for it but to fess up and deal with the fallout.

He moved his glass to buy a moment, then met her gaze. 'No. Actually, it's been over a year—'

'Over a *year*! Wow! That's a—' She blew out a breath, and then her gaze was clearing, brightening almost, which was bewildering to say the least. She straightened back up off her elbow, sipping more water. 'Then again, I suppose you *have* been *extremely* busy of late…'

Giving it all the emphasis, but meaning what, exactly? What was she trying to say? That he was busy with the band in a general sense, or that—

His chest went tight. 'I'm not too busy for my old mates, if that's what you're implying.'

Her glass went down. 'No, I—'

'I mean, yes. This last year *has* been hectic, but Carl has also got a phone. He has my number, could have—'

Stop!

Dumping on the hard-pressed Dr Valentine was not going to endear him to Izzy any, and it wasn't even the point, was it? The point—*the rub*—was this whole fame business, the way it skewed things. Perception. Image. *Everything*.

It was hard to take sometimes.

Oh, for sure he had used it, played up to the 'hot drummer' label, but what else was he supposed to do, post-Janine? Go to red carpet events and pose for photographs alone while Jaxon and the others were standing with their significant others—significant others who had *not* dumped them just days before they'd played the television show that had put them on the map?

No way! Easier to milk the myth, like he had at school. It wasn't a crime. Not now. Not then. What sixteen-year-old boy alive wouldn't have wanted to be viewed by his mates as a sexual kingpin? It had raised him up in their eyes, just as his lovely red carpet companions raised him up now in the eyes of the world. But in the *real* world, the one that truly mattered, the thought that anyone—*Izzy*—could think him so shallow as to not have time for a lifelong friend because he was too busy being famous was—

'Are you okay, Finn?'

Looking at him. Concern in her eyes. Curiosity. *Warmth...*

He forced a swallow. 'Yes, I was just...'

Her brows arched. 'Getting your dander up?'

Trying to get it under control more like, but she was close enough. Close enough to make denying it pointless.

He shrugged. 'Sort of, I guess.'

She shook her head at him, and then she was pushing her hair back, locking smudgy, sparkly eyes on his. 'I wasn't having a go. Really, I wasn't. You *have* been busy—for which, huge congratulations, by the way.' A smile touched her lips. 'It must be very exciting...'

That gaze... Hazel-soft, glowing.

His stomach shifted. How could he have read her so wrong?

Idiot, Finn! What was up with him, jumping at shadows, getting himself into a stew? He wasn't the reactive type. And yet he could feel something still whirring away inside him, chafing, because there was more to say, wasn't there? Context to explain—that he *must* explain—so she would know for certain that he wasn't a flake or all up himself now that he was a famous drummer in a famous band. He *had* to make her see, understand that he was a decent person, and maybe that was because he had never shown her that back in the day—who he really was inside—too damn worried about breaching the best-friend's-sister code to risk being even normally friendly. Or maybe it was just that fame had made him overly sensitive to this stuff—fact versus fiction—but whatever the reason, he had to get it off his chest.

He returned her smile. 'Thanks. It *is* very exciting, yes, but, getting back to Carl…'

She waved her hand. 'It's fine, honestly.'

'No, it isn't! I *need* you to know something.' He leaned his arms on the table to be nearer to her, fastening his eyes on hers so she would see he was being straight-up. 'Carl and I *do* keep in touch. We always have. But for years, probably since halfway through uni, it's been a bit hit-and-miss. It's got nothing to do with what's happened to me this past year. It's just life, you know, separate paths and all that, but it doesn't mean that we're not still solid, that we—'

'For goodness' sake, Finn. I *do* get it!' Cutting in, rolling her eyes. 'And also the first time as well.'

Nice one! Pushing her to the edge of irritation but worth it for clarity's sake.

He drew back, making his voice meek. 'Well, that's all I wanted. For you to get it.'

She gave a little shrug. 'Well, I do, so…'

Leaving him a handy gap.

'Could I just add—'

'Seriously? There's more?' Shaking her head, but her gaze was bordering on indulgent, drawing a smile up through him somehow.

'I just wanted to say that I *did* actually call Carl a couple of months ago but got his voicemail and no return call, my point being that he can be a very hard man to get hold of.'

Holding his gaze, on and on, and then suddenly her lips curved into a smile. 'You're right. He's a total nightmare. I never know whether he's on days or nights or pulling a double shift. He works crazy hours, and when he isn't working, he's sleeping. His life is insane!'

His veins tingled. But what of hers? Did he

dare ask? But then, how not to? How to even stop himself when the words were already in freefall?

'And what about your life, Izzy? What about you?'

'My life…?'

Because repeating the question was obviously going to buy her heaps of thinking time, wasn't it? Time she was already wasting on self-recrimination…

Why hadn't she just downed the water, thanked him and left straight away? That way she could have avoided awkward questions like this. *Why* had she let curiosity take her over, let herself fall for his amusing banter and twinkling eyes?

She dropped her gaze to escape his. Too much conspiring against her, that was why… His heroics for a start—rescuing her off that table, then more or less *carrying* her out here, his warm, deep smell beguiling her senses and her silly shoes barely touching the ground. And his kindness, ordering water for her, pouring it… Of course, the setting wasn't helping—romantic table on a romantic terrace, all the pretty lights above them and a glowing lantern between them, and the sea right there, lapping against the hulls of the boats in the marina, the sound of it soothing to her poor rakija head. It was fantasy stuff, a little bit of a very old dream come true—hardly incentive to speed-dial an escape cab.

Oh, and the irony was that she had been aware of the risk from the start, that he might know about the wedding and get to it at some point. It was why she had checked his gaze for clues in the bar, why she had asked him straight-up if he had spoken to Carl recently—the only way he could possibly have known—because if he knew about it, then she wanted to know, wanted *not* to be blindsided. And when he had said it was a year since he had spoken to Carl, *rejoice, rejoice...*

But she wasn't rejoicing now. Oh, maybe Finn didn't know about the actual wedding, but he knew something was up. His gaze just now, deep-diving, taking her apart. His gaze in the bar, full of questions—why was she out alone, drinking and dancing, flirting with rowdy guys? What had led her to it? And she didn't want to get into it with him, because no matter how lovely he was being right now, at school he had made her feel like a total loser—drawing hope up through her in the wings that day, only to dash it to pieces again, crushing her heart— and wasn't she already feeling like a big enough loser because of Eddie? Telling Finn the whole sorry tale would only amplify her pain a thousand times and she couldn't stand it, not when he had made it pretty clear in the bar that the only reason he was looking after her was because she was Carl's sister.

She bit her cheek. But she couldn't *not* answer, not give him something. Because even if it was only because of Carl, Finn *had* been decent to her tonight, *was* taking care of her. She owed him. And it would have to be the truth because for one thing, she was no good at lying, and for another, he would only find out from Carl anyway. And if he thought her a loser for getting herself jilted—or made her feel like one—then did it really matter? It wasn't as if she could sink any lower, and she would be leaving straight after, wouldn't be seeing him again.

The main thing was not to cry.

That she couldn't do—not in front of Finn.

Breathe.

She took hold of her glass, steeling herself, then raised her eyes to his. 'I think it would be fair to say that my life's a train wreck right now.'

'How come?'

Searching her face, concern in his gaze, and kindness, not a loser vibe in sight.

Way to make the ache start, the tingling burn. Throat. Eyes. But she would not cry, would *not* give in. Channelling the anger, that was the thing, using it to shape her tone, her delivery. Acid-bright.

'Well, you see, three days ago was my wedding day. A beautiful day—perfect weather. I had a lovely church with a lych-gate decked out in flowers, a gorgeous dress, everything a bride could wish for, really—oh, except for a groom.'

'What?' Finn's jaw went slack. 'He didn't turn up?'

Morning suit, crisp white shirt, that silk cravat, same perfect blue as his eyes...

She blinked the image away. 'Oh, he turned up, all right. He just couldn't quite get the vows out at the critical moment.'

Lips parting for words that never came...distance growing in his eyes...and silence, expanding...that feeling of dread rising and rising and rising...

She swallowed hard. 'It was quite the experience, I can tell you. Not at all humiliating. Whispers going round, minister whisking us off into the vestry to "take a moment". Bit of a change from taking vows, I suppose...'

And Eddie there, wringing his hands, pushing them through his pale red hair, giving it the works, the full-body plead. 'I'm sorry, Izzy, but I can't do this. It wouldn't be right. We're not in love...not in the way we should be. There's no spark between us. We're a habit, that's all. That's what we've become, and one of us has to have the guts to say it, to put an end to it.'

And there she had been, thinking it was their new beginning…

She sipped some water, swallowing it quickly to reset. 'Anyway, as everyone said afterwards, far better to put the brakes on *before* the wedding if that's how he felt. Personally, I'd have rather he did it before we got to the altar, you know, like *five* years beforehand would have been good, or six, or seven, before we…' Her heart twisted hard. 'Before *I* wasted all that time on him, invested so much in us. But maybe that's just me, being unreasonable, expecting too much. Who the hell knows?'

'Oh, Izzy, that's…'

Empathy, glistening in his eyes—*glistening!*—prodding at the ache inside her, filling her throat with a lump. She gulped down more water to clear it then parked her glass. Just one last thing. Then she was out of here.

'So, here I am, on my luxury honeymoon for one. Eddie said I should use the booking and obviously, whilst I'm not remotely interested in anything he has to say, since he forced his platinum card into my hand in lieu of a wedding ring, I thought, why the hell not? He's caused me some damage. Why not cause him some back?'

'Ah…' Recognition flared in Finn's gaze. 'The shoes.'

Oh, he was smart—smart as well as gorgeous.

If he had been anyone else, she'd have been giving him the serious come-on right now. As it was…

'Yes! Louboutins. To go with this designer dress. Gifts, courtesy of my *love*.' She felt a satisfying ripple of spite. 'And believe me, I haven't even started yet.'

Finn's mouth opened, then closed again, as if he had thought better of whatever it was he had been going to say. And then he sighed. 'I'm sorry. I don't have the words…'

Like everyone. But it was fine. She was done talking anyway, more than done with seeing this confusing warmth and empathy in his eyes. She had answered his question, paid her little debt of gratitude.

'Don't worry. No one does.' She reached for her bag. 'Look, I'm going to go now.'

He gave a slow nod, and then suddenly his eyes lit. 'Can I walk you back? Are you staying in town?'

If only… The second she had arrived, clapped eyes on all the loveliness she wouldn't be sharing with Eddie—the rustic terrace overlooking the sea, the vast bed with its gauzy white drapes, all of it even better than in the online photographs—she had tried to find something else, something in the noisy thick of things, but seemingly there was such a thing as *too* last-minute!

She got up, testing herself for steadiness. 'No. I wish I was, but the villa I booked is miles out— *secluded and romantic*, wouldn't you know—not that I'm bitter or anything.'

Although…strangely enough, at this moment she couldn't feel any actual bitterness. Maybe venting to Finn had done her some good.

'I'm quite a way out too, but I don't mind it.' Finn was up now as well, coming round to stand beside her. 'It was a good excuse to rent a motorcycle.'

Oh Lordy! A vision she could well do without: Finn in all his glory, straddling a motorbike!

Push past it, Izzy…

'So are you here on holiday then, or what?' Because *not* asking would seem weird and because also, even though she didn't want to be, she was a smidge curious.

'No, not on holiday…' He let out a wry chuckle. 'Although there're some who'd disagree with me.' His hand came to her elbow lightly, guiding her through the tables and out onto the pavement that ran along the marina. 'I'm actually here with the band. We're recording a new album.'

'Exciting!'

'It will be—when we actually get going with it.'

Implying what? Technical issues? Artistic differences?

Best not ask, though, if she ever wanted to get away, which she did, *must*! Because lovely as it was to be on the receiving end of all of this attentiveness, the warmth of his hand was messing with her pulse big time, stirring her senses around. And how could that even be happening when three days ago she had been set to commit herself body and soul to Eddie for the rest of her life, when she was *supposed to be* broken-hearted? How could she possibly have any bandwidth at all for Finn and his lovely warm hand when she was so…so…*consumed* by everything that had befallen her?

'So, this is me.' His hand fell away as he cruised over to a fine-looking black motorcycle parked by the kerb. He touched the handlebar lovingly, then looked up, his eyes twinkling. 'I've got room for a passenger if you want a lift.'

She felt her traitorous belly dipping. How would it feel to be sitting behind him, thighs cradling his hips closer than close, holding on tight, breeze blowing in her face, road blurring beneath them? Wild. Hot. Sexy. Thrilling.

Her insides quivered. *All of the above*. And exactly what she was craving, what she had set out expressly to find tonight. But not with him. Especially *not* with him.

Thankfully, the practicalities made it a moot point…

'Thanks for the offer, but I don't see a spare helmet anywhere.'

'Ah…' His gaze flicked to the bike, then came back to hers, all sheepish. 'You're right. Sorry. My bad.' He shook his head, then grinned. 'Note to self. In future, think things through *before* you open your mouth.' And then he was turning, scanning the marina road. 'I'll grab you a cab.'

As if she was suddenly his responsibility…

Could this really be the same Finn Falco who had backed away from her in the wings that day as if she had just sprouted two heads, as if he hadn't been staring at her the second before, filling her heart with hope? Could this Finn be the same one who had seemed to go out of his way to ignore her after that? In rehearsals. In the corridor. At home. Could this Finn, who had seemed so desperate for her to 'get' that he wasn't too starry for his friends now—as if it *really* mattered to him what she thought—be the same Finn who, at their leavers' ball, when she had gone all out in a red velvet dress and matching red lipstick, hoping to get his attention, had swept past her without a glance?

Her heart pulsed.

Oh God!

And why was she even doing this, dredging up the past? It was history—literally! Stupid teenage stuff. The world had moved on. They were adults now. *That* was why Finn was treating her right, or maybe it *was* because she was Carl's sister, and he felt some obligation. *Whatever!* His motivation, his business. She had *herself* to think about. And Eddie. The whole Eddie-Izzy debacle. Plenty of meat on those bones. More than enough to chew on without adding Finn to the mix. Drunken Izzy had had it right back there in the bar—Finn Falco was not, could not ever be part of her equation.

'Izzy…?'

Her heart jumped. Other than that he seemed to have found her a cab and was standing, holding the door open for her.

She thanked him and got in, meeting the driver's questing gaze. 'Paradise Villa, please. It's about a kilometre past the Horvat Estate sign…'

'Yeah, I know it.' He turned to set the meter.

'Will you be all right now, Iz?' Finn. Looking at her through the open door, his expression warm, open, *expectant*…

Her heart fluttered. What was he expecting, though—a get-together some other day? Was he waiting for her to suggest it?

Oh, the irony. But she couldn't entertain it, no matter how much the teenage Izzy inside her was jumping up and down begging her to, because seeing Finn again wasn't going to help anything. It would only mess with her head when it was already messed to the max because of Eddie. She had to do the wise thing and cut him loose.

She steadied herself with a breath, then nodded, making her tone warm. 'Yes, I will, thanks to you.'

And now, the awkward bit...

She settled back into her seat—surely enough of a signal—then reconnected with his gaze, keeping her own gaze level. 'I hope things go well with the recording process. I'll be sure to give the new album a listen when it comes out.' *And now, smile...* 'Goodbye, Finn.'

Confusion flickered through his gaze for an eternal, heart-tugging second, and then his lips flattened. 'Bye then.'

And then the door was shutting, and the cab was taking off, and she was done.

Done.

CHAPTER THREE

FINN SLEWED INTO the turning and pulled up in a cloud of dust, letting the engine idle.

Was he really going to do this, pitch up at Izzy's door after she had quite plainly given him the brush-off last night? Maybe it wasn't the best idea he'd ever had, but seriously—what did she *think* was going to happen? That he would take that cool goodbye lying down, let it stop him from calling by this morning to make sure she was all right? *No way!* For crying out loud, she was all alone on her honeymoon. Alone and sad. What kind of man would he be if he didn't care about that, if he didn't *want* to check on her? What kind of friend to Carl…?

He flipped up his visor to breathe better, felt his heart heaving. How could he not care, not come? This was Izzy, after all.

Izzy…

Who had blown him off.

His heart heaved a second time. If only he could make himself not care about *that*, make it stop plaguing him, hurting, but there it was. And now here he was again, sweating, getting hot under the collar just thinking about it. That calibrated goodbye smile, the finality in the word itself, loaded against him, putting him in his place.

He slumped back, wiping his palms on his jeans.

Why do that to him?

All night long, buzzing round and round inside his head. *Why? Why? Why?*

Hadn't he done right by her last night, looked after her? She had seemed grateful enough in patches, had seemed to be enjoying his company, lighting up at times, her eyes full of warmth that had felt genuine. But there had been retreating moments too, so many fluctuations in her mood that it got hard to keep up. And maybe that was down to the alcohol, or down to what her lunatic fiancé had done to her—which, fair play, was enough to throw anyone out of whack. Or maybe it was the weirdness of the situation that had thrown her, the two of them face-to-face again with only Carl and that potent, silent moment in the wings to share between them, which moment, come to think of it, together with its aftermath, might well have accounted for her initial frostiness…

That was, if she even remembered it, and if

he'd read the moment right in the first place, which he might not have. After all, Izzy had never given him any real indication that she liked him in *that way* so, it could be that everything he'd felt in that endless, tingling moment was down to himself and his own burning crush. For all he knew, she could have been gazing up into his eyes not because she was feeling anything but because she was trying to work out if he would ever let go of her arms. She might have walked away afterwards shaking her head, bemused at his bungling Mach 90 exit. If so, then her initial hostility last night couldn't have been related...

He blinked, absorbing the glinting green of the pines and the olive trees flanking the rough track before him, the soft grey crumble of the stone walls that separated track from vegetation.

So what was it, then, that had set her off at the start? Had she found him intrusive? Heavy-handed? Or had he simply been a proxy for that idiot, Eddie? A man! Ergo one of Eddie's kind, ergo eligible for a dose of sarky disdain.

Who knew?

Whatever it was, she had got over it pretty quickly once they were outside, hadn't she? Looking at him with those smudgy, sparkly eyes of hers, thanking him, being softer, warmer toward him. Opening up about her wedding, being feisty about it, but also welling up, sharing her pain with him, making his own chest ache, his eyes burn, making him want to scoop her up and protect her.

Stirring all that emotion inside him, only to go on and deal him that bruising goodbye…

His pulse struck up. Had he shown her too much empathy, perhaps, made her pain worse? That could happen. Like Jaxon…after Janine… giving him the doleful eyes, making the anguish inside him surge and throb, making him want to escape, hide. Had he made Izzy want to escape from him for that same reason?

He licked his lips. Or, clutching at straws now—had he unwittingly pushed her over some edge, freaked her out by offering to give her a ride home? Had she thought he was coming on to her?

The view ahead blurred.

Cripes… If so, she was wrong, couldn't have been *more* wrong!

Not that he didn't still fancy her, because he did. And not that, in between all the buzzing why-why-whys in his head last night, there hadn't been a voice too, whispering about how she was free now, and about how he was free as well, and about how this could be a chance for him. But that was only a remnant of the stupid teenager inside him, begging to be heard, not realising that Izzy would no more be looking to start a new relationship with anyone right now than he would be himself. The teenager inside him, forgetting that he had adopted a *no woman, no cry* policy, that he wasn't up for having his heart trashed again.

Trashed. Torn. Trampled.

Nice one, Janine!

Tearing them apart just days before 'Olive' had bagged the primetime music slot on Sam Nelligan's chat show that had changed their fortunes overnight. Leaving him just when he had needed her the most, to share the joy and excitement, to keep him grounded, keep him right. But no, she had ducked out just shy of the finish line, pouring scorn on his dreams as she went, calling him a fantasist, a man-child who couldn't commit to *real* life—a mortgage, marriage, kids— all the things she wanted.

Unfair! Because he did want those things. For pity's sake, he was all about family, family and everything it stood for. It was in his blood, in his DNA!

For sure, his own drove him crazy, talked over him all the time, but he wouldn't have it any other way, wanted a big noisy family of his own one day. But only when the time was right. And eighteen months into a long-distance relationship had *not* felt like the right time, not with the band finally finding a bit of limelight at the fringes, not when they had all worked so long and so hard for it, spent years playing in ropey dives up and down the country, hauling themselves and their equipment to rain-drenched, half-baked music festivals for that exact thing.

Making it *wasn't* a fantasy. It was *the plan*. Always had been. And Janine knew that, had come on board supporting it, supporting him. To turn tail and throw it in his face as she had, calling it a stupid pipe dream, trying to guilt trip him over it, was *not okay*. And if she had thought that stuff all along, had never really been real with him, then he was better off without her.

He rubbed his eyebrow. Didn't stop it stinging like hell at the time though, and the aftermath wasn't great either—being both famous and alone.

At least Izzy would be able to put herself out there again when she was ready, but he had lost that freedom, hadn't he? He was a *name* now, second hottest band member after Jaxon Cairns, according to some asinine social media poll.

He bent to the handlebars and set off again, keeping to low gear, allowing himself the luxury of a hefty sigh.

Way to make dating impossible! Well, maybe not dating as such—he wasn't short of attention in that respect. The problem was *believing* that the women who wanted to date him now wanted to date him for the right reasons, and not just because he was 'Finn Falco'. And it was hateful to be so mistrustful, because it wasn't his nature, and it wasn't respectful to women, either, to be always questioning their motives, but there it was. Relationship-wise, everything was harder now, close to impossible.

And he didn't want to be alone, living this topsy-turvy life without someone by his side who felt like home, someone he could make a home with. But between finding it inside himself to trust again, and getting to grips with this new reality—the recording and the touring, the events and the PR, the endless hotels and the difficult decisions, the constant motion that made even looking for a place of his own impossible— he just wasn't in any kind of shape to start something with anyone. Alone was the only way to be. The best, safest, easiest way to live.

So if Izzy had got it into her head that he had been trying it on last night, then she was way off the mark. His only thought had been to take care of her, see her home safely.

His breath caught. And now here it was, coming into view. Paradise Villa. Not a villa in the grand sense but a low rustic building with a weathered pantile roof, and bottle-green shutters, and a sitting-out terrace that probably over-looked the sea—hard to tell from this angle.

'Secluded and romantic, wouldn't you know...'

He pulled up, levering off his helmet. Izzy wasn't wrong about that. Trees all around. Birds flitting about. Blue, blue sky and the sound of the sea. He felt his nerves settling. *This* was special. His kind of place. In the thick of nature. Peaceful. Which Antonio's place was as well, but his estate was set higher, so the views were more open, stretching across vineyards and lavender fields to the sea beyond. This was prettier, cosier, a proper little haven.

Idyllic!

An idyll he was possibly about to ruin with his appearance.

But he wasn't turning back. How could he without seeing that Izzy was all right? How could he when it felt as if there was something between them that needed to be fixed?

Because leaving things the way they had last night wasn't right. Not after they had been getting along, when making her laugh had felt so damn magical. Not when she was out here all alone, for God's sake! Not when he was here, when fate had conspired to put them both in that bar *at the same time* last night—another freak-ery his mind had made ceaseless, pointless hay with in the wee small hours—when being here meant he could look out for her, be a friend to her. Surely she could do with a friend right now? A sounding board. Someone who could relate, someone who cared…

He re-tied his hair and swung off the bike. And he *did* care about Izzy. For good or ill she was tied to his past, and to Carl, and for that reason he was seeing this through. Not that he exactly knew what 'this' was, or what the hell he was actually going to say to her, but hopefully inspiration would strike. And who knew? Once she got over the shock, she might actually appreciate the aspirin he had brought in his backpack!

CHAPTER FOUR

IZZY OPENED HER eyes and winced. Were those rakija shots ever taking it out on her now, and had she thought to pack any painkillers?

She allowed herself a groan and rolled over, squinting into the spiralling brightness of the bedroom. Of course she hadn't. Packing, she had been too busy caressing all the sexy lingerie she had bought to surprise Eddie with, too busy fantasising about how she was going to spice up their flagging love life, to be thinking about analgesics.

She heeled her hand against her forehead to press out an ache.

Flagging...

How easily the word had dropped. Starkly true. *Sad.* But it didn't only apply to their love life, did it? She could apply it to date night too, and to their ambling Sunday afternoon walks, to picnics on the heath, and trips to the Tate Modern. All the things they used to do. Dwindling away. Their glue, shrinking. Eddie working late more often to make partner. She not even minding, actually liking coming home to peace and quiet and total command of the remote control. And of course, these past ten months, she had been planning the wedding, hadn't she?

Project Wedding! Her new raison d'être. Because the perfect wedding and honeymoon would be the perfect shot in the arm for her and Eddie, wouldn't it? And a honeymoon baby would glue them back together, boost them into a whole new exciting chapter…

Exciting.

She bit into her lip. There was another word. Not one she automatically associated with Eddie.

Her heart rolled. Sprang to mind like a jumping jack whenever she thought about Finn, though, didn't it? Which was only all the time since she couldn't seem to stop thinking about him now. That first blind-shock moment… *'For God's sake, Izzy, get down from there before you fall…'* That tingling moment by the bike… *'I've got room for a passenger if you want a lift…'* And then that last, terrible farewell…

Gah!

She threw off the quilt and got up, dragging on her robe. So much for being done. So much for imagining it was even possible.

That torturous taxi ride home… Gazing out at the glowing streets but seeing only his eyes, that wounded parting look. Staring at the dark shapes of trees and seeing only that flickering bewilderment. Playing it back on a loop, feeling wretched inside, confused, conflicted. Because Finn had hurt her plenty in the past, so what did it matter if she had hurt him back?

What did it matter?

She marched into the kitchen, yanked a bottle of water from the fridge and pressed it to her pounding head.

What did it matter?

Tossing and turning all night long, repeating the words over and over. *What did it matter?* But see, that was the thing about the old hurt. It wouldn't stick to this new Finn, this noble Finn who had saved her from falling, who had taken care of her, made her smile, made her laugh. Try as she might, and heaven help her she had tried, she couldn't make it stick to this Finn who had listened to her wedding woes with genuine sorrow in his eyes— *tears*—because this Finn didn't deserve it.

She rolled the bottle against her forehead. *That* was why it mattered. *That* was why she hadn't slept a wink, and not sleeping a wink on top of all the rakija was why her head was aching. And that was probably karma, siding with Finn, having the last laugh at her expense!

She screwed her eyes shut. So, what to do? She would only find peace if she made things right with him, but she didn't even know where he was staying. And if she ran the gauntlet of Carl's awkward questions to get Finn's number and called him, what would she actually say? She couldn't tell him the real reason she'd cut him loose last night, which left, what? Apologising for the way she had said goodbye while still saying goodbye, and somehow making it clear she was *still* set on not seeing him ag—

Holy moly, the doorbell!

She fumbled the bottle down and clutched at her robe, heart pounding.

Who the hell was it? Not a courier. She hadn't ordered anything. And it was way too early for her cab. Her spa session wasn't until this afternoon.

Oh God! Stranger danger. Yet another downside of being here all alone in the middle of nowhere. And now the bell was sounding again—a sustained finger push.

Determined!

She cast around quickly, seizing a tall wooden pepper mill off the worktop. Maybe it was ridiculous, arming herself like this, but if it came to it, she wasn't going down without a fight.

At the door she pulled in a breath, then opened up a crack.

'Good morning, Izzy.'

Oh my God. Finn!

Ripped jeans. Biker boots. Helmet in hand. Pack slung over one broad shoulder. Tentative gaze. Hesitant smile.

'Sorry for descending on you out of the blue like this...'

As well he should have been, given that he was basically ignoring the message she had taken pains to put across to him last night. Then again, that he wasn't an axe murderer was a point in his favour, as was how ridiculously hot he looked in those jeans. And his being here *did* present an opportunity to smooth things over, didn't it, in kind if not in words? What price pleasantness after all, if it lifted her guilt away, freed her mind to focus on what was really important? What price pleasantness when it was what he deserved?

She smiled to put him at ease. 'Please don't apologise. It's fine...' She opened the door wider, angling herself so he wouldn't see the stupid pepper mill. 'I don't quite get why you're here, though. And how did you even find me?'

His brows flashed. 'Not by any devious means, I promise. I heard you telling the cabbie you were close to the Horvat Estate, and that's actually where I'm staying. With the band, I mean...' He gave a little shrug. 'Antonio Horvat owns the place. He makes wine as well as music.'

So Finn was her next-door neighbour!

Comforting. Sort of. Maybe…

She refocused. 'So this Antonio is your producer?'

Segue to nowhere, but it was out of her discombobulated mouth now, courtesy of her discombobulated brain. Not that Finn seemed to mind. He was nodding, sliding his free hand into the back pocket of his jeans.

'Yeah. He's got a recording studio in one of the old wine vaults.' His eyes crinkled. 'It's pretty cool.'

'I'm sure.' Stone arches, curving cavernous spaces. Easy enough to imagine, but not the easiest topic to come back on.

And Finn wasn't helping any…

Too busy looking gorgeous in his *take-me-now* jeans and soft plaid shirt to throw something into the conversation. Too busy giving her tingles with his amber gaze, ticking boxes he had no business ticking, boxes that shouldn't even have been blank for him to tick. Which thoughts had nothing whatsoever to do with the subject in hand, which she needed to get back to, pronto! With something. *Anything!*

She fired up a smile and aimed it at him. 'What I mean is, it sounds like a fantastic space… Amazing. Awesome!'

His brows quirked. 'Impressive hyperbole.'

Desperate times, desperate measures more like, but she'd take it.

'Thanks.'

He smiled, his gaze settling. 'As to *why* I'm here, I just wanted to check you were okay today.'

Her heart crumpled. Way to add fuel to her guilt. Coming to check on her *in spite* of how she had said goodbye to him last night. Coming as if the hurt she had seen in his eyes—*definitely seen*—hadn't been there at all. Coming regardless, like a decent, caring, noble—

'And also…'

Her crumpled heart thumped. 'Also what, Finn?'

Looking at her, teasing his lip with his teeth, and then his gaze fell, as if he was searching for the words. And she wanted to help him, say something encouraging, even though encouraging him was also the very last thing she should do, but before she could even straighten that thought out in her head, his eyes were lifting again, pinning her gently. 'Look, Iz, could I maybe come in for a moment?'

Oh Lordy!

Coming in was next-level. Coming in wasn't seeing him off with a smile and a lightened conscience, was it? But what to do? He was here now, holding her to ransom with his eyes, had come to check on her, a kindly gesture which surely called for some reciprocal kindness, some decency on her part. But she wasn't prepared. Not emotionally. And definitely not physically, standing here as she was, in this scanty robe with not a stitch on underneath, clutching a hulking great pepper mill.

'Izzy, please…?'

Oh no! And now his gaze was flickering with bewilderment, same as last night, tugging at her heart strings all over again and she couldn't bear it, couldn't bear the thought of hurting him again by saying no. Which left only one option…

She licked her lips quickly and smiled, stepping back. 'Sorry, yes, of course. Please, come in.'

'Thank you.'

But was Izzy *genuinely* okay about this? Or had he pushed her too hard? And what was he even doing, asking to come in when he had only the haziest notion of what he wanted to say to her? When it was all emotional froth and nonsense inside him. A pointless, shapeless muddle that had one foot in the past and one foot in the present, with no walking legs attached, and no final destination, because what final destination could there possibly be with Izzy?

He closed the door, glancing about him to buy a moment, only half taking in whitewashed walls, pale stone flags. A console table. A bentwood chair.

He should have quit while he was ahead, contented himself with the knowledge that she was alive and well and knew where he was staying now, should she need him in an emergency. But no. He just had to go the extra inch, didn't he? Push for more. Give himself over to the magnetic pull of her. And now here he was, stranded in her hallway, trying to hold it together while simultaneously trying not to notice her curves beneath that exotic, silky, super-short little robe she had on, and all he could think of to say was…

'Nice hall.'

'Yes. I mean, it does the job.' She gave a small smile, and then she was backstepping, blushing a little, holding her robe in an awkward one-handed grip. 'So, would you like some coffee?'

His heart rose. Having coffee together was bound to smooth things out, give him some much-needed thinking time too.

He smiled. 'Thanks, sounds great.'

'Okay, kitchen first then.' She pressed her lips together and pivoted, treating him to a compelling view of her shapely calves and her sleek thighs and—

What the…?

He felt his eyes widen. 'Is that a pepper mill?'

Her stride faltered. Then she was rounding on him, eyeing him with a comically defiant gaze. 'Yes, it is, as it happens.'

He felt an inkling stirring, an irresistible spark of mischief igniting.

He touched his chest. 'Geez, I'm sorry, Iz. Were you in the middle of making breakfast or something?'

Her chin lifted. 'No.' And then suddenly, as if she couldn't be bothered hiding the obvious anymore, she gave a little shrug. 'I just wasn't expecting anyone, so I thought I'd better—'

'Arm yourself with a pepper mill?'

Her eyes narrowed. 'Don't you laugh at me, Finn Falco.'

'I'm not.' He shrank back to seem scared. 'I wouldn't dare...' Not on the outside, anyway. On the inside, different story, because what sight in the world could be more amusing than this one: Izzy, scowling, facing off against him, clutching a pepper mill that was longer than the robe she had on. Maybe it would backfire, but he couldn't stop himself, couldn't resist.

He raised his helmet to his head slowly, willing the laughter he could feel vibrating inside him to stay put. 'If you don't mind, though, I'm just going to put this back on...'

Her scowl tightened, but then her lips were twitching, curving upwards into a wicked smile. 'Good luck with that.' And then she was bringing up the pepper mill, slapping it against her hand, her eyes glinting with menace. 'Because this baby's good and hefty, has a nice *long* reach...'

His stomach kinked. God help him, he couldn't hold in his laughter now. It was rumbling up and out of him, and it felt so good to be laughing like this, seeing laughter sparking in her eyes too.

He took a backwards step. 'Should I be afraid?'

She dropped her chin. 'Oh yes...' And then suddenly she was lunging at him, dancing him backwards, pepper mill jabbing the air, words coming out with every thrusting jab. 'You. Should. Be. Very. Afraid.'

Too much! He could feel a stitch biting into his side, his knees trying to buckle. Too hard to defend himself when he was laughing like this. He fumbled his helmet and pack to the floor and held up his hands, crossing his forefingers.

'Pax, okay. Pax!'

She came to a breathless stop, eyes shining victorious. 'Pax? You're pleading pax? What are we, kids in the playground?' And then, as if her own words had just caught up with her, she let out an irresistible, helpless giggle. 'Oh God, we're exactly that, aren't we? Behaving just like kids...'

Laughing like kids, playing like kids, feeling light and joyful like kids.

Balm for the soul.

He let his hands drop. 'So what, if it feels good? Maybe we should all give in to silliness more, let the inner child in us out to play more.'

'That's very deep.'

Teasing him with her eyes, filling his well.

He felt his cheeks creasing. 'What can I say? I'm a deep kind of guy.'

'Who's no closer to getting that cup of coffee...'

'It's cool.'

'Remiss, more like.' She frowned, then offered up the peppermill. 'Do you mind taking this?'

'Not at all.' Because how could he deny her anything when her robe was parting so delectably, giving him a rather nice view of the dusky hollow between her breasts, which maybe she caught, because in the next moment she was turning, tightening her robe back up, setting off along the hall.

'Come on!'

He followed her, entering into a light, airy kitchen modelled along rustic Mediterranean lines, not that he had much time to take it in before she spun round.

'I'll make you a coffee, but then, if you don't mind, I'll go get dressed.' She flicked a glance at her robe. 'As you can see, I wasn't expecting company.'

Timely reminder!

Perhaps he should apologise...

'I'm sorry, Iz. And of course I don't mind…' He felt a tingle, an idea coming. 'In fact, since I'm the one imposing, and since I also lost the battle of the pepper mill, why don't *I* make the coffee while you go sort yourself out?'

She tilted her head over. 'You'd do that?'

Warmth in her gaze, like the warmth she'd been putting out last night before that foxing goodbye—the goodbye that was all muddled up in the reason he was standing here right now, muddled up in the tangle of whys and wherefores. *Although*…did they matter anymore after the pepper mill? Did they count anymore now that he and Izzy were in this lighter, easier zone?

His chest tightened. The thing was though, she had let him in to hear what he had to say, hadn't she, so when that moment arrived, he would have to…

He refocused. A problem for later. Right now, he needed to reply to her question.

'Of course I would.' He parked the pepper mill and smiled. 'It's the least I can do.'

Her eyes smiled back. 'Okay, well, thanks.' And then she was stepping back, gesturing expansively. 'Make yourself at home, okay? It's lovely out on the terrace if you want to go see.'

'Thanks.'

She smiled again, and then she turned toward

the door, disappearing through it, and he was alone.

He inhaled to centre himself, then scanned the room. Wooden cupboards. Pale marble worktops. Coffee machine—one of those types that took little pods.

Last resort!

He set about searching the cupboards. This close to Italy—Pa's own country—there surely had to be…

Bingo!

One silver espresso pot. What about coffee, though?

Fridge!

He pulled open doors, looking for the one that would reveal the—

Seriously…?

He felt his shoulders sagging, his eyes staring at two bottles of champagne, three bottles of water and absolutely nothing else. No milk. No coffee.

No food!

He let the door close, felt his chest tightening again.

This wouldn't do. Maybe Izzy was struggling to eat because she was upset—which he got because after Janine, he had been the same—but she needed something, especially after last night.

His heart fluttered. Would she take it the

wrong way if he were to…? And if he did, would that be involving himself too much?

He scrubbed at his lip. But no. *No!* It was only what Carl would do if he were here. So he would only be doing the same as Carl. In fact, Carl would *want* him to do it, look after Izzy. His heart fluttered again. Did he even have enough time, though?

He went back into the hall and held his breath, listening. Shower was going, splashing away.

Good!

He might just manage it if he left now.

Helmet.

Check!

Pack.

Check!

Door key…?

On the side table.

He picked it up, slipping it into his back pocket, then made a silent exit, finally giving in to the smile he could feel rising. With a bit of luck, he'd be back and fully set up before Izzy even knew he had gone.

CHAPTER FIVE

Izzy twisted up her hair and stuck in a clasp.

What did Finn want to say to her? Asking to come in so he could say it, yet here she was, showered and dressed now, still none the wiser because ten seconds through the door, he had somehow changed the landscape…

'Is that a pepper mill?'

She felt her traitorous lips curving upwards for the hundredth time. That adorable, mirthful catch in his voice. *Infectious!* Making her smile. And she had tried to hide it because self-defence was serious, not a laughing matter, but then he had got her with that helmet gag. Broken her.

Impossible not to rise to it, and it had felt so natural and easy, in spite of the past. Spontaneous. Like they were on the same beat, riding the same bright, tingling wave…

Bittersweet.

A taste of what they could have been together. *What you could still be…*

She squeezed her eyes shut. No. *No!*

How could she even be thinking such a thing when she was this fresh off the slab, still bruised and bleeding, thinking it about Finn, of all people…?

Chief high school tart! Playboy rock star drummer!

Yes, he had a heart of gold, demonstrably, but he'd broken hers once, so even flirting with the notion of letting him in, letting herself like him—*trust him*—was utter madness. In fact, trust was off the table, period. With anyone. Because even Eddie—who was nothing like Finn, so dependable and straight that Carl used to call him 'steady Eddie'—had let her down, hadn't he? At the altar, no less, dressing it up as having guts!

Eddie…

Her first and only boyfriend. The only man she had ever been with. And she had once thought that was so great, hadn't she? Defending herself vehemently to Carl when he had pulled her aside at her engagement party to challenge her sanity, telling her twenty-one was too young to be tying herself down—as if he even knew anything about love and commitment, perpetual singleton that he was.

How glorious it had felt putting him in his place, knocking down his objections one by one.

Why *should* she date other people when Eddie

was perfect? Why play the field, waste her time and her body on others, when she had already found her lobster, when she and Eddie were golden, when Eddie looked at *her* with such love in his eyes, when Mum and Dad adored Eddie and his parents to bits, when their two families gelled, when everything in their garden was rosy?

Her heart pinched. At least Carl had had the good grace not to remind her of that self-righteous little tirade when he had driven her to the airport, but would she ever find an equal grace inside herself to admit to him that he had been right? Because he had been, must have been. Otherwise she wouldn't be here now, trying to work out how her garden had gone from rosy to rose-tinted, how she could have missed her and Eddie's sell-by date flying past.

She met her own eyes in the mirror. At least, that's what she should have been doing, analysing her ten-year engagement, trying to find closure, but instead she was trying *not* to think about Finn in his soft shirt and ripped jeans. Trying *not* to think about how it had felt to laugh with him just now, feeling light and loose and electric. And especially, she was trying not to think about how her body had tingled when his gaze had slipped into the folds of her robe. She had to stop these thoughts coming because Finn was *not* a prospect. He wasn't one of those guys in the bar, wasn't random—far from it. He was her teenage crush and the author of her teenage misery. He was a player and always had been, famous now, hanging out on planet rock star with other famous rock stars, and models, and actors—the whole kit and glitterati caboodle. Kind he might have been as well, but he was not for entertaining, not for thinking about, not for even one more second!

She turned toward the bedroom door. For sanity's sake, she had to go back, hear him out, then get rid of him—politely, warmly, graciously, but firmly—so she could stop going round and round in these silly pointless circles and focus on herself, which was, after all, why she had come on honeymoon alone in the first place.

No sign of him in the kitchen.

No sign of him in the sitting room.

Terrace?

She padded along the hall and out through the French doors, and there he was, turning from the view to meet her gaze, breaking into his beautiful, easy smile.

'At last!' He came forward. 'I was about to send out a search party.'

What to say? Taking time to choose the right dress had seemed important.

'I'm sorry, I was—'

Her heart stopped.

What was all this food doing on the table? Filo pastries. Croissants. Fresh figs. Smooth-skinned persimmons. Cheeses. Cold cuts. Orange juice. And coffee. One of those espresso pots she saw everywhere but didn't know how to use. All this, and not from her kitchen because…

Oh God!

Way to melt her heart into a giant Finn-shaped puddle.

She lifted her gaze to his, battling the sudden hot ache behind her lids. 'You went out for this.'

He nodded. 'I had to.' He smiled again, pulling out a chair, motioning her into it. 'In case you haven't noticed, your fridge is—'

'Empty. I know. Thank you so much…' She sat, pulling her napkin onto her lap, because *yes!* he'd covered that base too. 'I just haven't been feeling hungry.'

'I figured.' He sat down opposite, his gaze tentative suddenly. 'You don't mind that I did this, do you? I mean, I don't want you to think I'm being—' His lips came together. 'I just think you should eat something.'

She looked at him. All this kindness. Yanking at strings, wreaking havoc. But she couldn't let it show. All she needed to convey was simple, heartfelt gratitude…

'Of course I don't mind.' She smiled. 'How

could I, when you've been so thoughtful?' She looked at the food, felt another smile bubbling up, effortless this time. 'You seem to have bought everything in the shop.'

He grinned. 'There wasn't time to shop. I raided the fridge at Horvat's place.'

'So your poor bandmates are now starving because of me?'

'Hardly. The fridge up there's the size of a hangar.' He flicked a glance at the table. 'So dig in, because I'm serious. You *need* to eat.

'I think I've covered most of the bases— veggie, vegan, gluten-free—so you should be okay, although—' panic flared in his eyes '—I'm not sure about nuts. Are you—'

'No! I'm not allergic…' Crumpling like paper in the face of his kindness, yes. Allergic, no. 'You're looking at a girl who eats peanut butter from the jar.'

His eyes sparked. 'You do that too?' Then he was chuckling, reaching for the coffee-pot. 'Smooth or crunchy, though?'

'Per-leaze! It can *only* be crunchy.'

'Thank God.' Pouring. Smiling. 'After the pepper mill, I wasn't relishing the thought of going another round with you.' He set the pot back down. 'So, what can I get you now? Milk with that? Aspirin, maybe?'

What?

She looked at him. 'Aspirin?'

'Yeah.' He drew a box into view, setting it down in front of her. 'As an aficionado of the hangover, I figured it might hit the spot.'

She felt a catch in her chest. Was he actually trying to kill her with kindness? Because seriously, she was dying here, panicking now, because he was doing everything right. *Everything!* Making her like him, and she didn't *want* to like him. Not in the way she could feel herself liking him. Not when the other shoe was suspended, likely to drop. Because that other shoe always dropped sooner or later, didn't it, causing pain, be it in the wings of a high school stage or at the altar, and she couldn't face it again. She needed not to be in this situation, feeling this confusion, which meant moving things along, and quickly.

'Thanks, Finn…' She took two caplets, then shot him a smile, because she *was* grateful, and he deserved to feel that from her before she put him on the spot. But it had to be done. Carpe diem and all that. She inhaled to steady herself. 'So, now we're set, are you going to tell me what you couldn't tell me on the doorstep?'

His heart missed a beat.

Oh God!

How could he have ridden to and from Antonio's, filled and emptied his backpack, laid the table, found napkins, made coffee, *and* remembered to put the aspirin on the table just in case, and still *not* straightened all this out in his mind?

Too busy being thrilled at the thought of surprising her, that was why. Too caught up in delight to jump his mind through all the tricky hoops.

And now she was reaching for a croissant, regarding him with that wide hazel gaze of hers, and he wanted to be honest, tell her she had hurt him with the way she'd said goodbye last night, tell her that it had felt like a kick in the teeth after he had gone all out to look after her and he wanted to know what he had done to deserve it.

But if he was *that* honest, then he would have to explain *why* he had been going all out. And if he started unravelling that thread, getting into how last night had felt like a way to make amends for backing away from her in the wings that day and ignoring her ever afterwards, then he would have to go on and explain why he'd done *that*, explain how it was misdirection to hide his feelings for her from Carl—*huge crush feelings*—because he didn't want Carl to know, to think he was switching to Izzy's camp. Because Carl was his friend, the only one who listened to him banging on about his music dreams without that same sceptical look in his eyes he saw in everyone else's, and he just couldn't risk losing that, messing up that friendship.

Idiotic, no doubt, but that was just how it had been back then. How it was even to this day, since he had never told Carl about his crush on Izzy, had never quite felt the urge to tell him.

Probably because ten seconds after Izzy got to uni, she took up with Eddie, then got herself engaged to the guy ten seconds after graduating...

Different lives. Different directions. Water under the bridge. So far under that he would have been happy to fess it all up for the sake of context. Except...what if she thought he was *still* crushing on her, and was trying to open a door?

His heart spasmed. Way to freak her out, spoil this nice thing they had going on.

He lifted his cup to buy time. There *had* to be a way to be truthful with her, a way to find out why she had pushed him away last night that wouldn't get him all snarled up, give her the wrong idea about why he was here.

Then suddenly he had it.

Of course...

The bike! The lift!

If it came to it, he could pull that cord. It was the perfect solution!

If only it made the plunging in part easier...

'It's not so much *telling* you, Izzy, as, well...' He sipped to steel himself, then set his cup down. 'It's about last night. About the way you said goodbye.'

Her hands stilled midway through tearing off a piece of croissant, her cheeks colouring as if he had struck a nerve.

So there *had* been something in it! But she wasn't jumping in to speak. And so…

'I felt… What it felt like…' Damn his own cheeks growing warm now, the hurt biting again, but he had to push through. 'Frankly, Izzy, what it felt like was the *brush-off*, and I couldn't see why you would—'

Wetness in her eyes. Very slight. Just at the edges.

Oh God!

Making her cry wasn't the aim. He wanted answers, but not at any cost. Not at *this* cost.

Bail, buddy, bail!

He licked his lips quickly. 'And then it came to me that it was probably all *my* fault for offering you a lift, that maybe it came across the wrong way, got you thinking I was coming on to you, and so you felt you had to send me a message?'

Blinking now, biting her lips, reaching for her coffee, but she still wasn't saying anything.

His heart pulsed. Was he on the right track or the wrong one?

'To be clear, I *wasn't* coming onto you, Izzy. It was just a lift. Because you were a bit worse

for wear, and you'd been upset, and because—
helmet oversight aside—offering to see you
home felt like the right thing to do...'

Blinking. Sipping.

Still not saying anything...

'So, that's it, in a nutshell. All I wanted to
say...'

Geez!

Was she ever going to cut him a break? Re-
spond?

Maybe a touch of humour would shake her
loose.

He reached for his cup again. 'Of course, if
you blew me off because you can't stand the
sight of me, then fair play.'

Her cup went down with a clatter. 'I *wasn't*
blowing you off, Finn!' And then her gaze faltered and fell. 'Oh, goddammit!' She let out a
sigh and looked up again, her throat working.
'And now I'm lying...'

'So you *were*?'

'Yes! But it wasn't anything to do with the
lift.' Her brow wrinkled. 'You didn't come over
like a creep, so you can stop worrying about
that.'

Small mercies!

He parked his cup. 'So what should I be worrying about? I mean, if you blew me off, you
had a reason, right?'

She turned away, chewing her lips again, as if she was trying to think of how to phrase whatever she had to say, putting his guts through the mill in the process. Then her eyes came back, hazel-soft, troubled.

'Look, this isn't the easiest thing to say because we're not exactly friends, but at the same time, you've been acting like one—like a kind, good, lovely friend—so I'm going to tell you, confide in you, *as a friend...*' She ran a tongue across her lip. 'I gave you the brush-off last night because I don't want you cramping my style.'

The words circled.

'I'm sorry—what?'

'I *said*, I don't want you cramping my style.'

'No, I got the words—just not the meaning.'

Her lashes fluttered. 'No, well, you wouldn't, because I need to explain, don't I?' She swallowed, drawing in a little breath. 'First, I want you to know that I appreciate everything you did for me last night. I'd have fallen off that table for sure if you hadn't intervened.' Another breath. 'The thing is, though, by intervening, you also kind of messed things up for me.'

Messed.

Things.

Up.

Her gaze flared. 'I can see I've lost you, but you'll get it in a second.' She lifted her cup and sipped, eyes eternally locked on his, and then she set it back down again with a sigh. 'Here's the thing. I wasn't only dancing in that bar last night. I was out on the pull.'

'The pull?'

'Yes! You know…' She clapped a vertical hand to her forehead. 'Sharking.'

'I know what it means, Izzy, I'm just…'

Gobsmacked.

And yet it made sense. That dress. The way she had been dancing. *Those guys.* He felt his chest tightening. In truth, wasn't it partly why he had launched in? Not only to save her from falling but also to keep her out of the drunken arms of one of those lumbering oafs, because the thought of her ending up with one of them was simply—

Her voice broke in.

'You needn't look so shocked. You're a man of the world. Surely you understand?'

Defiance in her eyes now, in her pout.

'I want some of what you've been having for years, Finn, because I never have. I met Eddie in my first year at uni, then got engaged three months after my finals. I've never been with anyone else, and now I want to. Intend to!' Her eyes flashed with an evangelical light. 'I want to do all the things I've never done. I want to go crazy. Let go. Have fun. I want to have a fling!

A no-strings, no-holds-barred holiday fling. And I'm sorry, but when you put me in that taxi last night, I sensed you wanted us to get together again and if I misread that then, apologies, but that's how it felt. All I could think was that I've got ten days of honeymoon left, boxes to tick elsewhere, and so…'

'You gave me the shove.'

She nodded, but then her expression was collapsing, fervour gone. 'If it helps at all, I felt wretched about it afterwards, didn't sleep last night because of it. In fact, full disclosure, just before you arrived, I'd been about to phone Carl to get your number so I could call you to apologise.' Her voice dipped, catching a little. 'When I opened the door, I have to say, I was pleased to see you.'

Which he had felt, hadn't he?

But it didn't change the picture. Didn't change that she was set on having a so-called good time with someone else, someone she hadn't even met yet, someone she was going to let kiss her and touch her, put their hands—

Stop!

What was he doing, riling himself up, feeling possessive?

He didn't own her, had no stake here, didn't even want one! None of his business if she wanted to let loose after Eddie, have some fun.

His heart clutched. Except it wouldn't be fun, would it? He knew it, because he'd had a one-night stand once. Not countless times with countless women as per the myth, the myth Izzy had clearly bought into, but once, and once had been more than enough to know it wasn't for him.

What was so great about intimacy followed by emptiness? *That* was the reality. Lying there breathless, feeling warm and spent and utterly, utterly alone. Might as well service yourself!

He looked at her. Was that really what she wanted, sex without connection?

He felt his heart turning over. It couldn't be. Not little Izzy Valentine. Izzy, who couldn't walk a straight line in her Louboutins, who had jousted him to his knees with her pepper mill and her laughing eyes, who ate peanut butter from the jar just like he did.

He didn't know her, no, but who she was inside was right there in her eyes. If she went with some random guy, she would feel deathly miserable afterwards, he knew it. Worse than he had, since she was pinning so much on it. And maybe he didn't have, or want, a stake, in this, but he did care about her. And if she considered him a friend now, then wasn't it his duty as a friend to pass on his experience, make her think twice...?

He felt a tingle. And wouldn't sharing be in

the open spirit of the moment, too? Oh, for sure, there were things he would have rather been sharing with her. A tour around the island on his motorbike, for example. A swim, communing with the fish, or an al fresco lunch at that swanky beach club up the coast, the one with the billowing white curtains and the incredible view. But those things weren't on the table, and so...

He shrugged to break back into the moment. 'Well, at least you were pleased to see me.'

Her face split with a smile. 'How do you do that?'

'Do what?'

'Make me smile so easily?'

Magic light in her eyes, stealing his breath away. Not helpful when he needed breath to speak with, when he had important things to say.

He shrugged again. 'Who knows? Maybe you're just easily amused.'

Her lips curved again, then twisted sideways. 'I *do* feel terrible about last night.'

'Don't.' Because it was behind them now, not worth dwelling on, whereas this... He fastened his eyes on hers. 'Look, Iz, in the spirit of friendship, can I say something?'

'Of course.'

'It's about what you said earlier, about wanting what I've been having for years.' He swallowed. 'You know it's all nonsense, right? Mythical.'

Her lips parted. 'Mythical? But you're…' Staring into his eyes. 'I mean, at school you were—'

'A terrible flirt, a serial dater, but in reality, somewhat chaste.'

'Chaste!' She barked out a laugh. 'Are you having me on? Also, who uses that word these days?'

He felt a twitch about the mouth. 'That would be my mother.'

'But you had such a reputation!'

'I know.'

'And you didn't mind?'

'No. I was a teenage boy. Sexual prowess was like, kudos.'

Her gaze narrowed, accusing. 'So you just let *people* believe you were something you weren't?'

'Yeah. It was dumb, but then, teenage boys *are* dumb, ruled by a different compass.' One that had made confessing his feelings to her in the wings that day seem impossible. But this wasn't the moment to be thinking about that… 'What I'm trying to say is that I'm not the fast and loose type and never have been, so if you think you're using me as a template for what you want to do, then you're not. In fact, full disclosure…' Mirroring her own vocabulary seemed apt. 'I've only ever had one hookup in my life, and that's because I didn't enjoy it.'

Her brow wrinkled. 'Why? Wasn't it crazy hot?'

Slamming back against the door. Kissing. Hands hot. Everywhere. Diving under his shirt, between his legs, seizing, unzipping. Bed, rising up beneath him. Himself, crashing down. Head, whiskey spinning...

He shook himself. 'At the start, maybe, although we were both drunk so, you know, beer goggles and all that.'

Izzy reached for a fig, her eyes never leaving his. 'When was this? How did it happen?'

'First year of uni. I'd just been dumped by my girlfriend, so not quite your situation, but a baby version of it. I was at a party, getting wasted, and met this girl. She started kissing me, making moves, so I thought, why not? I took her back to my room. She launched herself at me, ripped some of my clothes off, got on top.'

Skirt up around her thighs. Condom fumble. Wham-bam, straight to it...

'It was over in a rush. She crashed out beside me, fell asleep, and I just stared at the ceiling with my head spinning, feeling like crap.' He poured himself some more coffee to give the image time to grow in her mind, then carried on. 'When I woke up, she was gone. I never saw her again, never even knew her name, but the feeling stayed with me.'

'You felt guilty?'

'No! The sex was consensual, but it was also

the single emptiest experience of my life so, not the easiest thing to forget.' He felt a flick of devilment and went with it. 'That's not to say you won't have a blast, but the casual hookup thing, personally, I wouldn't recommend it.'

'Hmph.' She frowned, then looked down at her plate, taking a knife to her fig. 'Sounds like you were probably a bit *too* drunk.'

That was her takeaway? The drunkenness, *not* the randomness, or the total absence of emotional connection? *Unless...* Unless this was just bravado, Izzy not wanting to admit her plan was a bad idea. Tied in with her determinedly downturned gaze, didn't it, the laser focus she was applying to that fig, the colour that was creeping into her cheeks?

He felt a stir inside, a sudden wave of satisfaction.

He had made her think. Got to her! Which perhaps made this the perfect moment to leave. Give her space to reflect…

His stomach shifted. Give himself space too. Because if he had got to her, it was no more than she had done to him, *was doing* at this very moment, getting to him with her lowered gaze and that smooth, sweet curve of her cheek, loose golden strands grazing her neck and the white straps of her sundress. He could feel tenderness aching in his chest just looking at her, his hand wanting to slide over hers. and he couldn't be doing with feeling these things, not in the way he was feeling them, not in this deep, yearning way.

It was one thing being a friend to Izzy, quite another caring about her. But he couldn't let those two strands start twisting into something else, because that would only mess him up, make him vulnerable, and he couldn't afford to be vulnerable around Izzy, not when, for a million and one reasons, this was a going-nowhere situation.

He needed to leave. Keep his distance going forward.

Izzy would likely appreciate that, in any case.

He picked up his cup and drained it, then got to his feet, keeping his tone light, casual. 'Izzy, I need to scoot, get back to the guys.'

Her head jerked up. 'But you didn't eat anything!'

'I ate earlier.'

'Oh…' Her gaze flickered. Then she was flattening her hands on the table, making to rise. 'Okay, well, I'll see you—'

He flashed his palm to stay her. 'No, please.' Easier to leave her here with the soft breeze shushing in the trees and the view of the sparkling turquoise sea just down the slope than to struggle through an awkward goodbye at the door. 'I'll see myself out.'

'All right. If you're sure.' She dropped back

down again, then her eyes lifted to his. 'Thanks again, for everything, Finn.' Softness filled her gaze. 'Also, thank you for sharing.'

'No problem.'

Unlike breathing suddenly.

He shook himself, mustering a smile as he turned toward the French doors. 'You know where I am if you need me. I'll leave my number in case of emergencies.' Which hopefully signalled his intention not to reappear otherwise, but he wasn't looking back to see if she had got it, because if he did, found himself trapped inside her gaze again, then, God help him, he might never get free.

CHAPTER SIX

WHAT A COMPLETE waste of Eddie's money that
was! Full-body massage, deluxe facial, pedicure,
manicure—the works. All for nothing because
she wasn't remotely soothed and relaxed.

Izzy rammed on her sunglasses and pushed
out through the pristine glass doors.

Finn's fault!

For upending her this morning, leaving all her
preconceptions about him high and dry.

How had they even got to *that* revelation?

She stirred herself to walk, not seeing the
quaint, narrow street, not caring where it led.

Her own doing… Pressing him to say what
he had come inside to say but hadn't got to yet.
Pressing him to push things along, so she could
be done with him and his confusing kindness.

So much for that plan! What she had got was
Finn, telling her she had hurt him with her goodbye last night, dragging all her wretchedness
back to the surface, then doubling it by taking
the blame onto himself for possibly spooking her

with his offer of a lift—so wide of the mark it wasn't true. And while she had been busy trying to process that, wondering what to say, he had made that joke at his own expense about her blowing him off because she couldn't stand the sight of him, and she had felt her veins bubbling because that wasn't true either, was the very *opposite* of true! And she had meant to say that, but in the muddling froth of the moment, what had come out of her mouth was, *'I* wasn't *blowing you off, Finn!'* which she'd had to take back immediately because lying to him after he had been so sweet and lovely to her simply wasn't on.

The pivotal moment…

Finn, coming back at her with wounded eyes and *why?*

Only she couldn't tell him the truth, that she had pushed him away because she had been in love with him at school and couldn't handle the confusion of being around him again, especially when he was being nice to her now, warm and protective, and looked better than ever.

So she had clutched at a sudden, desperate straw instead, told him she had given him the push because she didn't want him cramping her style.

Vaguely true at least, in that it had definitely crossed her mind at some blurry point last night. And it had felt like a neat way to declare her agenda, drive a wedge between them under the guise of friendship. And for a scant second or two, it had felt liberating, speaking up for herself for once, laying out her needs and desires and intentions like a confident person, seeing the shock all over his face. Better, though—*admit it*—was unburdening herself to him about how wretched she had felt for the way she had said goodbye, seeing how the light in his eyes changed, softening…

Oh God!

But then he had dropped his bomb. He wasn't a player, was, in fact, the total opposite! A man who needed to feel an emotional connection with his lover. A man blessed with possibly more than a few romantic bones in that divine, honed body of his—which, heaven help her, made him even more attractive than he was already. A man who had opened up to her about the misery of his one and only one-night stand to sway her from her chosen path. Not preaching. Not judging. Simply sharing.

Then leaving. In a way that signalled he wouldn't be back.

Which was desirable. Perfect, in fact. Except, what was she supposed to do now?

Her original plan for today had been spa, bar, then whatever transpired with whomever, but now…

She paused. Stone steps. Descending to a narrow alley. At the end of it, a patch of sparking blue sea. She pulled in a breath and set off again, heading down, sandal slaps echoing off the craggy walls either side.

Now she was up the creek sans paddle! Not only sans paddle but with her brain on fire into the bargain because it wouldn't stop thinking that Finn must surely care about her to have opened up to her like that, that if he didn't care, he wouldn't have bothered trying, however subtly, to dissuade her from getting involved in a casual encounter which he clearly sensed—*how?*—wouldn't sit well with her in the end. Also, he wouldn't have bothered coming to check on her earlier, coming *in spite of* her brush-off, if he didn't care, would he? And he *definitely* wouldn't have troubled himself going back to Antonio's to fetch breakfast for her. Breakfast *plus* aspirin!

Such kindness. Such care. *Actions* not words, which always spoke louder, spoke to some affinity he felt for her perhaps, and how tantalising a thought was that...?

Her heart plunged. Oh, but then *there* was the problem she had always had with Finn, her eagerness to seize on a tantalising thought and spin it into fool's gold. Imagining she could feel his eyes on her face when she was singing during those rehearsals, imagining it in the corridor when she was talking to her friends, *sensing* it so strongly, like a message he was sending out, that when she had bounded into him in the dark curtain folds of the wings that day, felt his hands catching her arms, so firm and quick, she had imagined herself some longing into his gaze, hadn't she? Felt it melting her, lifting her, but she had got it wrong. All of it. Because he had let her go and cut out at lightning speed, had never met her gaze again, which was the writing on the wall right there. Great big letters!

Yet here she was again, a grown-up now who should have known better, filling Finn's kind acts with romantic fantasy elements, adding bonus features when he had made it perfectly clear, had taken considerable pains, in fact, to point out to her, that the lift he had been offering was nothing more than that. Not a come-on. Not a romantic overture. Just a lift. Because it had felt like 'the right thing to do'.

Think about it! Everything he had done for her lined up through that lens. Rescuing her off that table, sobering her up, coming to check on her this morning, bringing her breakfast and aspirin, cautioning her against the lonely fallout of a casual hookup, leaving his number scrawled on a pad in case of emergencies. But also leaving.

Think about it! Leaving in a way that signalled he wouldn't be back.

Gah!

As if any of it mattered, anyway. As if she didn't have significantly more important things to think about!

Enough!

Because here was the harbour now, opening out.

She drew up, letting her eyes take it in properly, because yesterday she had been too set on getting herself into that bar, too full of fight and fury, too focused on her agenda, to stop and look around her. And later, when she had come outside with Finn, it had been dark. But now…

Now here it was. A wide horseshoe harbour surrounded by low tree-covered hills. A perfect natural port, wrapped around with wide pavements and pale stone buildings, old and slightly jaded, slightly crumbling, but utterly charming with their pantile roofs and wooden shutters. Little shops. Restaurants and bars. Tables with merry parasols. A church with a bell tower poking up. An ancient grey castle overseeing everything from its elevated vantage point—the people coming and going, the palm trees rustling their fronds, and the sea, of course, blinding turquoise as ever, bobbing with boats, sparkling in the sunshine.

Beautiful...

She pulled in a breath and set off again, making for the stretch where the bars and restaurants were. Not that she wanted a drink. It would only reload her headache. And in any case—*admit it*—the only reason she had gone overboard with the rakija last night was to put herself into an oblivious state for a hookup because sober, she'd never have been able to go through with it. And whether Finn had sensed it in her because he had her inner track, or whether he had laid it out simply because it was the right thing to do, he had succeeded, turned her off the whole stupid idea.

She wasn't the casual hookup type. It was just an idea she had seized on to put off dealing with the debacle of the wedding. To put off asking herself how she could have spent the past ten months planning a wedding—catching herself up in a million pointless, finicky details, pinning all her hope on it, pinning notions of a baby on it, a baby that would give her time off from her going-nowhere job—even while she could feel the walls around her crumbling. But she couldn't avoid the question now, or the answer, which was that clearly, she had been living her life in denial, living it with her idiot head stuck in the sand!

She bit her lip, considering the kiosk up ahead. For such grim epiphanies as this, ice cream had surely been invented.

She bought a double chocolate cone and went to sit on the harbour wall.

Eddie was right to slam the brakes on. They had been running on fumes for too long, weren't in love anymore, not in the way they should have been.

She looked down into the glinting water. Had they ever been in love in the right way?

Eddie, at uni. Tall, fair, handsome. Smiling. Inviting her and some other friends to spend New Year at his rather grand home in rural Surrey. Dancing that night. Fast. Slow. Blue eyes, holding hers. Warm hands, holding her waist. And when he kissed her, it had felt like the world was opening up, falling into place. She had felt confident suddenly, like Carl was, like he had always been. Taller somehow, with Eddie by her side. Brighter. Better. It had felt so good that she had thought the feeling must be love. Not a tortured crush love but proper, grown-up love. Everything easy between them, companionable and safe.

And no one who mattered had said a word to dissuade her of it!

Her flatmates, Claire and Sal, swooning every time Eddie came in. *'He's so gorgeous, Iz!'*

Mum and Dad, glowing with approval every time she took him home. And Grandma. *'What a lovely young man, Izzy.'*

Everyone loved Eddie. And his parents loved *her* and her parents.

All of them dropping hints by their third year at uni…

'So, when are you two going to make it official, then?'

Her chest tightened. Was *that* why Eddie had proposed so soon after they'd graduated, because Molly and Eddie Sr were egging him on, because they were tight with her own parents, because the four of them had become the very best of friends? Trips together. Eurostar to Paris. Champagne selfies. Thick as thieves. Better than not getting on, but had Eddie felt pressured to propose?

Oh, that moment though… His great grandmother's ring. Handed down. Diamonds sliding onto her finger. Such joy! The feeling that she had achieved something at last, found her place, was worth something. Engaged! Not only that but starting her dream job at Archibald Fitz Advertising, the only agency she had wanted to work for. And Eddie had got articles at Sterling Hatt & Shaw, *the* top corporate law firm in London. And his folks had had the flat in Chelsea that *of course* they should live in, and it had all drawn together so quickly and neatly, everyone delighted except for Carl, sticking his interfering oar in at their engagement party. She had thought he was being mean about her and Eddie because he was jealous, irked that, for once, she was in the fast lane, pulling ahead, while he was behind, still slogging away at uni, still a student.

She felt a hot wave travelling up her spine, shame prickling in her cheeks.

So wrong!

Carl had seen it all, somehow, the mistake she was making with Eddie, the spark that was missing. The spark that would have got them excitedly setting a date within a year or two instead of languishing, ticking off the years, revolving but not advancing. The spark that would have at least got them talking about *why* they weren't pushing for the finish line. Instead, the push had come from their parents…

'Are we ever going to have a wedding? Hear the patter of tiny feet?'

So they had finally set a date, kicked into gear. At least, she had. Got stuck in. Got it into her head that it was just the happy reboot they needed, the very thing that would make—

'Watch out! You're dripping.'

Her heart lurched.

Oh no!

Ice cream. All over her dress. And Finn— *Finn!*—standing there, shirt unbuttoned loosely over his tee, sunglasses glinting, wayward strands of his hair catching the breeze.

Her heart lurched lower, into the very pit of her stomach.

Here? *How?* And how did he always get to look like a Nordic god while she was flailing around in the active throes of some epic fail?

'Here, let me...' He came forward, relieving her of the cone, holding it at arm's length. 'Sit tight while I ditch this.'

'Okay.' Because what else was she going to do in a white dress dotted with suspicious brown splodges in the lap area?

She found a tissue in her bag and set to with it, blotting, but it was no good. Then Finn was back, pulling a squashed half-empty bottle of water from his back pocket.

'Is this any use?'

Chocolate teapot came to mind. But the offer was kindly meant.

She shook her head, pushing her shades up to let him into her gaze. 'Thanks, but I think it might just spread the stains.' *You might also want to say...* 'Hello, by the way.'

'Hi.' He smiled briefly, hesitated for a beat, then sat down beside her, pushing up his own sunglasses with a silver-ringed thumb. 'A pain about your dress.'

The least of her worries, one of which was Finn himself, being here, hesitating before he sat down as if it was a weighty decision. And there was her own reaction to contend with too, the completely irksome and unwelcome tingle that was running through her because he had made that decision, and the equally irksome compulsion she was suddenly feeling to be winsome and wryly amusing for him. But there it was…

'Yeah. It's not great, but it beats being jilted at the altar so, you know…'

He let out a gratifying chuckle. 'Now that you put it like that…' His eyes came fully to hers. 'So, what are you doing in town?'

'I was at the spa, being pampered.'

'Figures.'

'How come?'

'You smell nice.'

Very candid! And not at all making the moment as sticky as her dress, not only for her but seemingly for himself too, if the sudden touch of colour brightening his cheeks was anything to go by.

She forced up a quick smile to rescue them both. 'Thanks, and what about you—what brings you to the metropolis?'

'The bike's got a slow puncture. I took it back to the rental place. They're fixing it just now.'

'So, you're killing time.'

'Yeah.' His eyes flicked to the water. 'I was looking out for fish, hoping to spot a big one.'

His brows rose. 'You'll say if I'm in your way or anything?'

Her ribs went tight.

Unsubtle much!

Checking in to see if she was still set on her hookup plan.

She bit into her cheek. If she pretended that she was, then he would take off, which was obviously the most desirable outcome. But lying to him didn't seem right, not when he had rescued her from the clutches of a leaking ice cream cone. Besides, what if he started up again, trying to dissuade her? Then she would be stuck defending a position she wasn't even interested in taking, and frankly, she just didn't have the steam for it!

She permitted herself a sigh. 'You're not in my way, Finn, not *cramping my style*, if that's what you're getting at. For one thing, I've got no style left to cramp. For another, I've axed my agenda.'

His lips parted. 'So, you're not…?'

'No. Not sharking. Not on the pull. Just sitting here, dripping ice cream on my dress.'

He gave a slow nod, not saying anything, which somehow felt like a prompt, or maybe it was just that she suddenly needed to talk, offload.

'I think I was just lashing out, you know. At Eddie, with his credit card. At myself for… I don't know. Being blind. Sticking my head in the sand. It was all just a self-destructive adrenaline rush, but it's over now.' And to give Finn his due… 'Your timely words of wisdom played a part.'

The corners of his mouth lifted. 'I'll take "timely words of wisdom" over interfering any day.'

'You weren't interfering. You were trying to stop me doing something reckless which, I can tell you now, I'd *definitely* have regretted because I'm *not* the casual type. Not remotely. Which you'll have, of course, gathered from my very long and ultimately fruitless engagement to Eddie!'

He flashed a dimple. Then he was shifting, angling his body round a little more to face her, setting his bottle down on the wall between them. 'So, what's the plan now?'

What indeed?

'Breathing, I guess. Taking stock.' Her heart clenched. 'Making lists.'

'Lists?'

'Dividing up the spoils. For moving out.'

'*You're* moving out?' Disbelief in his eyes. 'Why *you* when he was the one that—'

'Because his parents own the flat.'

'Oh.'

Frowning now, piecing together what had

hit her like a ten-ton truck the second she had stepped into Paradise Villa—that when she got back, she'd be homeless, without even a shred of equity to her name.

His gaze reconnected. 'So, what'll you do? Go home to your folks?'

'I guess.' Although how that was going to work, *feel*, God only knew. Bad enough stewing in her own misery without coming up against Mum and Dad's. And what about their friendship with Molly and Eddie Sr? Would it survive, and if it did—

'You don't look convinced.'

She felt a scoff slipping out. 'Well, that's probably because I'm thirty-one years old and hadn't exactly planned on moving back home. Aside from the fundamental awkwardness of it, the commute into work from there is going to add hours to my week.'

His gaze narrowed a little. 'Graphic design, right?'

If he was changing to the subject to lighten her mood, then he had picked the wrong subject.

She held in a sigh. 'Yes. I'm on the graphic design team at Archibald Fitz Advertising.'

'And you hate it.'

'Is it *that* obvious?'

'Let's just say I'm picking up a vibe.' His chin dipped. 'Why do you hate it?'

Warmth in his eyes, interest, kindness.

She felt a flutter in her chest. How was this happening? How was she sitting here, talking to Finn like a friend? Liking it!

Was it okay to be liking it?

Then again, what did it matter?

It was only talking. Offloading. And Finn had time to kill, was asking the questions. So why not carry on? Who knew? He might put a different spin on things for her.

She shifted round, angling herself to face him fully. 'I hate it because I don't feel valued. I haven't moved up while my colleagues have. I'm doing exactly the same thing now as when I started.'

'Which is what, exactly?'

'Putting flesh on the bones of *other people's* ideas. I don't even know if I've got it in me to do more, or *be* more, but I'd been steeling myself to talk to my boss about a promotion, a senior designer position, so I could work more directly with the account execs on generating concepts. Then we set a date for the wedding, and I got distracted with all the planning. And I had my parents in my ear all the time, going on about starting a family, and to be honest, because there *is* such a thing as the biological clock, it seemed that a career break could be in the cards. So I *didn't* go to see my boss, didn't have the talk, and now here I am, still stuck in a job I hate. I've got to move back home, at least while I find a place to rent in town that I can actually afford, and even as I'm saying this, I'm not even sure that I *want* to be in London anymore, or in advertising either…' Which was one hell of an epiphany to be having mid-flow.

But it was true. She could feel the dead weight certainty of it sinking through her like a stone. London. Advertising. As of now, *not* the dream! And if she didn't even have *that* dream to cling to anymore, then what was left?

What. Was. Left.

CHAPTER SEVEN

GOD HELP HIM, how much did he want to put his arms around her right now? Hold her close and soothe her, breathe in her lovely smell that he hadn't meant to mention but had somehow.

A small slip. But putting his arms around her would be a fatal error, would play to all his weaknesses and he couldn't put himself in that position. Not after putting himself in this one. Stopping to help her out with that ice cream because he simply couldn't make himself walk past as if it wasn't happening. Sitting down beside her because leaving didn't feel right, even though leaving immediately would have been in his best interests.

And now he was stuck. Floundering. Victim of his own nature and his upbringing, wanting to help her, but how?

He couldn't fix her life, her job, her living arrangements. For pity's sake, he was adrift himself at the moment, sofa surfing until he could draw breath and buy a place of his own. He couldn't magic up stability for her, or certainty.

All he had, all he could offer, was a friendly ear and the thing he was actually thinking…

He dipped his chin, seeking her sight line. 'For what it's worth, there are a couple of things *I'm* sure of, Izzy.'

Her gaze reanimated. 'What things?'

'First, I'm one hundred percent sure that you need to give yourself a break, *stop* thinking for a while and just have a holiday.'

'A holiday?'

'Yeah. I mean, not to depress you or anything, but everything that's messing with your head right now will still be there in two weeks' time. But in two weeks' time, you won't have all this…' He turned to look across the bay to make the point, following the tree-line to where the houses started, then onward to the spread of the town, past the waterfront shops and bars, all the way to the ice cream kiosk where she must have bought her disastrous cone. Then he looked at her again. 'You should let it in, try to let it distract you. Give your mind a rest. Then maybe all the things you're not sure about will resolve themselves…' He felt a tingle. 'You know, like a crossword clue you can't get. You put it aside, go do something else, and when you come back, you see it right away.'

'You do crosswords?'

So *not* what he had expected her to come back

with, but her mouth was twitching a little, which was a sign of life, of merriment.

Heartening!

He smiled. 'No. *I* don't, but my Grandmother O'Shea does. Many a time I've seen her throw a newspaper down in disgust because she's stuck, then later she'll pick it up and be like, "Now there, Finn, would you look at that. It's only gone and come to me while I was puttin' the washing on."'

Izzy snickered into her hand. 'You might not do crosswords, but you do a very good Irish accent.'

'I should hope so after all the exposure I've had. I mean, Ma's from County Kerry. And we used to spend quite a few of our summers there when I was little, staying on my grandparents' farm.'

'Their farm?' Surprise in her eyes, then a smile. 'Wow, that's… Did you like it? What kind of farm?'

'Dairy. And yes, I loved it.' Velvet green fields. Romping with sticks. Low afternoon sun, and the herd ambling in for milking, Grandpa O'Shea whistling to the dogs, his brothers and sisters cavorting about, making their usual noise… His heart went soft. 'I think I fell in love with the great outdoors because of those summers. We were so free there, freer than at home. We'd spend the whole day outside, making dens in the woods, building dams in the stream, fall-ing in more often than not, going back covered in mud, getting an earful for it…'

'It sounds idyllic.' She chuckled a bit. 'The freedom, I mean, not the earful. Didn't you spend a summer in Italy, too?' Blushing now, for some reason, and then she swallowed, gave a little shrug. 'I mean, I seem to remember Carl missing you being around.'

'Yeah. So that would have been when I was seventeen. I went to stay with Pa's family in Tus-cany to help out in their hotel. It was work expe-rience, and a way to polish my Italian…' He felt his cheeks creasing. 'I was mischievous, though, persuaded my uncle to lend me his scooter which, of course, he didn't get back the whole time I was there.'

'So that's where the motorbike bug bit you?'

'No. I was born with the bug, just never got to indulge it before that summer.' He couldn't hold in a chuckle. 'I thought I was really some-thing, buzzing about with my cousin Emilio, hitting the village hot spots, which weren't that hot, to be honest, but it didn't matter. It was all about the wheels.'

She smiled. 'You've had a nice upbringing. I can tell.'

Warmth in her gaze, reaching all the way in-side him, stirring up thoughts and feelings he didn't want, couldn't afford to be having. Luckily, he had the perfect distraction tucked up his sleeve…

'Yeah, I've been lucky with my family, noisy siblings aside.'

'Noisy?'

'I'm being polite.' He pulled in a quick breath. 'So, do you want to hear about the other thing I'm sure of?'

Her gaze went still, then she laughed. 'Can you believe I'd forgotten that you had *a couple* of things…?'

He opened his palms. 'Witness the magical power of distraction!'

She scowled, giving him the playful side-eye. 'You're a menace, Finn Falco.'

'But you still want to hear, right?'

She rolled her eyes. 'Of course I do.'

'Okay, well, the second thing I'm absolutely sure of is that you could do with some ice cream.'

Her gaze solidified. 'Are you trying to be funny?'

'No!' *The look on her face…* 'I'm deadly serious. You lost out, and I think we should fix that.'

'But look at me!' She flicked a baleful glance at her dress. 'I can't walk across the street like this. I look as if I've had a very different sort of accident.'

'It's fine. I have a solution.'

'Please don't say it's to jump in the sea to

wash it off, or to drop my shades and pretend like nothing's wrong.'

'Okay, I won't.' Because what he had was so much better. He got up, shucking off his shirt, and held it out. 'Here. This should be long enough to cover your embarrassment.'

Her eyes widened. 'Your shirt?' And then she erupted into a smile that knocked the air from his lungs. 'You're an absolute angel, Finn. Thank you so much.' Sliding her arms into the sleeves, standing up, flapping the cuffs, giggling. 'How long *are* your arms?'

'Thankfully long enough to reach my hands.'

She paused for a second, then burst into giggles, eyes sparkling. 'You're so funny. So kind.'

Funny, and kind, and in serious danger of forgetting that nothing could happen between them, that she was fresh from the altar, in no place to start anything with him, and that he was too wary now after Janine, too surrounded by chaos to start anything with her. But he had better remember it, and also remember that Izzy was still Carl's sister.

Good pep talk!

He scooped up his water bottle, cramming it back into his pocket. 'Thanks, but the shirt was a no-brainer, bar the sleeve length.'

'Easily fixed.' She rolled up the cuffs with deft fingers and arranged her bag across her body, frisking her hands over the shirt-dress combo. 'Now, with a pair of red Doc Martens on, I reckon this could actually be an outfit.' She made a little preening turn, then flicked him a look. 'What do you think?'

As if he could articulate anything coherently right now! She might have been in sandals, not Docs, but regardless, the faded red of his shirt over the white of her dress was a very fetching combination, or maybe it was simply Izzy who was fetching.

Whatever!

He needed to reply, which might be easier if they were moving. Talking and moving. Another perfect combo.

He dropped his shades. 'You'd probably know more about that than I would. I'm not so into fashion, as you can probably tell. Shall we…?' He took a step, motioning for her walk. 'You look cute, though.' Because how could he *not* say it when she had probably seen it all over his face anyway?

Her cheeks flushed. 'Thanks.' And then she was falling in beside him, tipping him a glance. 'But you would say that, even if I didn't, because you're nice. And what's all this about not being into fashion? You're rocking the ripped jeans look.'

His heart spun.

Rocking? As in, a compliment?

'Thanks…' He smiled, only just managing

to keep it on the right side of goofy. 'I'll take that. But so you know, it's not a look. My jeans are ripped because they've done hard labour. The rips in the knees are from years of kneeling down to set cables, and these higher up ones are from a jagged edge on one of the crates we used to use for our gear. Got me so many times!'

Her hand went up. 'Hold the bus.' And then she was turning, looking at him with a quizzical expression. 'Exactly how long have you had those jeans?'

'A while.'

'As in…?' Arching her eyebrows, as if he ought to have documented all this stuff on a spreadsheet.

'I don't know. Five years, maybe.'

'That's…' Her gaze dipped, then lifted again, a teasing glint visible. 'Can I just check? Do you know that you're in a very successful band?'

Tactfully framed…

'I do. And yes, I *could* buy new ones, but I don't want to because I like these…' Oh, and now here was the perfect comeback sparking inside him, a little bit flirty perhaps, but she'd started it, so why not join in, have some fun?

He dug his thumbs into his pockets, the way photographers always asked him to do in photoshoots, then he looked at her through his shades, cocking an eyebrow, deadpanning for all he was worth. 'And since I'm apparently rocking these, why the hell would I want change them?'

Oh God!

Were they flirting now? It felt like it. Like fun with a tingling edge. Exhilarating, scary, and all her fault for working his shirt like a model, inviting him to comment on how she looked in it.

Not working it to flirt, but only to seem less discombobulated by the shirt-off-his-back gesture, by the worn-in softness and clean soap smell of the shirt itself, the intimacy of its enfolding warmth that was Finn's warmth, his body's warmth. It had seemed like an upbeat, confident way to deal with the situation. But then he had said she looked cute, discombobulating her all over again, because she would have died to hear him say that back in the day. And all she could think was that she needed to put the focus back on him fast. So she had said he was rocking his jeans—which was insane! Tantamount to admitting that she had noticed, assessed, liked. And now he was turning it back on her, chuckling behind his shades, laughing with his whole body, same as when she had gone after him with the pepper mill, and the moment was just too gorgeous.

But she couldn't stay inside it, couldn't give in to all the tingling sparks that were flying around because none of this was real. Finn was being adorable, yes, but he was also only doing the right thing again, wasn't he?

That hesitation in him before he had sat down on the wall back there—that was the giveaway. He had wanted to go, then thought better of it, stayed against his inclinations. And she was glad he had, because she'd needed to talk. And it had been nice listening to his stories. It was nice being with him right now, laughing like this. But she was someone he was looking after—his friend, Carl's sister, that was all—so best not get herself tangled up in pointless confusion. Best to bring them to heel with a change of subject. A nice, safe, neutral subject. That was, once she had given him the reaction he was clearly waiting for…

'Walked into that one, didn't I?'

'C'mon.' Opening his arms out, laughing. 'It was an open goal. You left me no choice.'

'Fine! Very deft. Very funny. Can we go get ice cream now?'

'Of course.'

He turned to walk, and she fell into step beside him. 'So, where's home for you these days? LA? New York? The Bahamas?'

He made a little scoffing noise. 'I *wish*. Hang on a sec…' He darted to a nearby bin, throwing in his water bottle, giving her an eyeful of his perfectly sculpted jeans-clad rear in the process.

Then he was back, shooting her a smile. 'So, actually, I'm currently homeless.'

What?

Way to take her mind off his tush!

She looked at him. 'Seriously?'

'Yes, but you needn't look so alarmed. I don't mean I'm *homeless*, homeless, as in, I've got nowhere at all to go. But I'm essentially a nomad at the moment, sofa surfing with family when I'm home. Not that I've been home much lately. Since we 'broke through', the band's been nonstop. Touring and all that, moving from one hotel to another. Sometimes rented apartments.' His sunglasses glinted in her direction. 'It's ironic, you know. For years, I couldn't afford to buy a place and now I *can* afford it, I'm never still for long enough to actually look for one. And like you, I don't quite know where I want to be yet, which doesn't help.'

'But you must have had a place before, right?'

'You mean back when I was working for BioOnica? Yeah. I rented a place just outside Cambridge, quite close to the lab, but it was no great shakes. It wasn't worth holding on to if I was never going to be there, so I gave it up.'

Talking as if she knew about his job, but she didn't. Either Carl had never mentioned it, or she hadn't been listening when he did, or maybe she had subconsciously blocked it out because of the past…

'I'm sorry, Finn. I'm embarrassed to say that I don't know who BioOnica are, or what you did there.'

'Don't sweat it.' His mouth twitched with a wry smile. 'It's not as if I ever did.' He was drawing to a halt now, pushing his shades up because somehow, they were at the ice cream kiosk. 'So what's it to be? Chocolate again, or something less indelible?'

She felt warmth flooding in. Such a lovely, lovely way he had about him.

'Chocolate again, please, but I'll take it in one of those cups this time.'

One eyebrow lifted. 'Playing it safe?'

'Too right. I'm wearing *your* shirt, remember.'

He laughed, then turned to the vendor. 'One large cup of chocolate, please, and one large pistachio.'

Her breath checked.

Large?

'No, Finn. Please. Not large…' Because the cup the girl was busy filling was freaking *enormous*. 'It'll be too much.'

'There's no such thing as too much ice cream, Izzy.' His eyes pinned her for a twinkling beat. 'According to my three-year-old niece, Maisie, anyway, and she's the expert.'

Her heart gave.

Adorable!

The idea of Finn taking his three-year-old niece for ice-cream.

And now he was handing her a mile-high stack of the stuff impaled with a small wooden spoon, his gaze glowing amber, making her heart give all over again.

'There you go. That'll sort you out.'

'Thank you.'

'You're welcome.' Smiling into her eyes, on and on, until suddenly he whipped his gaze away, looking along the pavement. 'Shall we go grab that bench?'

'Sounds good...' Because walking—*movement*—would be the perfect antidote to whatever *that* just was. Getting back to the subject of BioOnica would, too.

She set off beside him, popping a spoonful of ice cream into her mouth. 'So, you were telling me about BioOnica...?'

'Oh, yeah.' He glanced over. 'Okay, so BioOnica researches and develops drugs that target brain cancers.'

She felt a tingle, a detail coming back. 'You did biological sciences at uni, right?'

'Correct.'

And now here was the bench. They sat down, Finn parking himself not too close to her, thank goodness, and then he carried on.

'I was on the clinical trials team. Just a lab technician. I'm not saying that in a sad way, by the way. It was nine to five, paid the bills, and that was all I needed it to be.'

'Because you wanted to focus on the band?'

'Exactly!' He smiled. 'I wanted work that was interesting but not all-consuming. It suited me—'

But a ringtone cut him off.

'Sorry…' He pulled out his phone, glancing at the screen as he rose to his feet. 'It's the bike place.'

Calling to let him know his bike was ready, no doubt, which meant he would be leaving now. And it shouldn't have mattered one little bit, but it did. She didn't want him to go, couldn't help not wanting him to go. Because even if he was only hanging out with her to be decent, he was still nice to be around. Charming. Sweet. Funny. The best company ever. And kind.

She pressed her teeth into her lip. So kind that if she were to ask him to give her a lift to the villa on the back of his bike, just to see how it would feel, to experience it, he undoubtedly would…

But no.

No!

She dug her spoon into her ice cream. What the hell was wrong with her? She couldn't ask him. For one thing, he had been more than good enough to her already, and for another, riding pillion behind Finn, with all the associated holding on, would only fan the old flames, make her more susceptible to him than she was already and she didn't want that! Not when the pull of him was already *this* strong, when he was constantly catching her out with his smile and his delightful revelations. His grandparents' farm. His Italian uncle's scooter. His jeans that were old favourites and not a fashion statement. *Maisie!*

Finn Falco was the last tangle she needed to be getting herself into when she was still reeling from her wedding day fiasco, reckoning up all the years she had wasted clinging blindly to Eddie, thinking theirs was the marrying kind of love. When she was still trying to piece it all together, piece *herself* together, her whys and wherefores, faults and failings. When she was still bruised, and confounded, and hurting.

She held in a sigh. Maybe it was the hurt to blame, the hurt that was making Finn's warmth feel like balm to the soul, like a solid branch she wanted to reach for. But Eddie's warmth had felt like balm to the soul too once, had got her thinking, believing, that what they had together was special. Real.

And this was Finn, after all, who had snapped her heart in two at sixteen without a single word exchanged between them. Granted, he probably didn't know he had, was clearly a sweet and lovely soul these days, but even so, letting herself get too close to him, *motorbike close*, would be foolish.

Madness!

And here he was again, his smile at half-mast.

'The good news is that the bike's sorted. The bad news is that they're closing in T minus ten minutes, so I need to split now if I want to get it back today.'

She felt her heart bottoming out in spite of herself, forced up a smile to hide it. 'You must go then. Fly like the wind!'

'I'll need to.' He made to leave, but then he faltered. 'Will you be okay, Iz?'

Holding her gaze, his, full of warmth and caring, but she couldn't let herself bathe in it. He needed to get going, and she didn't need the confusion.

She freshened her smile. 'Of course. I've got sunshine and all this lovely ice cream. What more could a girl want?'

His eyes crinkled. 'You and Maisie would *so* hit it off.' Then he was striding away, chuckling, throwing up a hand. 'See you around, Izzy.'

Her heart paused.

Would he, though? Or was it just a figure of speech?

She looked down to load her spoon, felt her heart pausing a second time. Then again, if he wanted his shirt back…

CHAPTER EIGHT

'You got the bike sorted then, Finbo?'

Jax. Eyeing him from one of the four giant cream sofas arranged around the vast low table in the loggia.

'I did.' As well as losing his shirt to Izzy, and possibly more as well. But he wasn't going *there* with Jax, not when he could barely go there himself—how much he had loved being with her this afternoon, feeling those sparks flying between them, how crushed he had felt when he'd had to leave—when he didn't know what to think about that, let alone what to do about it. Jax would only recycle Finn's angst into a brand-new song, thieving magpie that he was!

Finn navigated around the table to the opposite sofa and sank down, meeting the now-famous blue gaze. 'Any progress yourself today?'

'Dribs and drabs.' Jax pushed both of his hands through his blond mop. 'I think we're nearly there with "Beholden to You". It just needs a bit more twang. No, not twang. More…'

He frowned, dropping his hands. 'I'll know it when I hear it. I'm going back in just now to work on it.' His brows lifted. 'Do you want to come?'

'Sure. Not that I'm an expert on *twang*…' But he did need to show his face now and again, keep in touch with what was being hatched. Besides, getting involved would help to keep his mind off Izzy. 'Are the others in there already?'

'Nah. Matt's gone for a walk. Taylor and Dobs are in the pool, drowning each other, with any luck.'

It was for this reason he stayed away.

'Right.' Jax got to his feet. 'Let's go.'

'Okay.' He went to rise, but in the same instant, his phone rang.

Carl!

Returning his call at last? Or calling to tell him Izzy's dismal news? Either way, they were going to end up talking about Izzy.

He swiped right, signalling to Jax to go on ahead. 'Hey, Dr Valentine! So you haven't struck me off after all.'

'Thank you, Finn…' That familiar dry tone. 'Never grows old.'

Same old Carl!

He grinned. 'Unlike time, buddy. Did you actually *pick up* the voicemail I left you a couple of months ago?'

'Yeah. Sorry. I was at work when it came in, was going to call you back. Then blah, blah, blah, excuses, excuses. I'm a bad friend. You should drop me.'

'I know, but see, I'm too nice to do it.'

'Still nice, huh?' Carl chortled. 'So you haven't turned into a diva yet? No pet chameleons with diamond collars?'

'Just the one.'

'Glad to hear it. Seriously, though, how the hell are you, Finn? A rock star now, no less! Is the dream all it's cracked up to be? Are you happy? Where actually *are* you at the moment?'

His heart rippled. Clearly Izzy and Carl hadn't spoken, then, which meant he had better answer the questions in order, because when he got to the last one...

He got up, moving to edge of the loggia, letting his eyes run through Antonio's lavender fields. 'I'm fine in myself...' *Current confusion aside*. 'Playing is great. Reaching bigger audiences is great. Glasto was a blast, and the Brits—what a night!'

'Three gongs, was it?'

He felt a smile breaking. 'Three we never expected. It was unreal. Brilliant!'

'It's a brilliant album.'

'Thanks. The fame thing is an adjustment, though. And you know that Janine bailed—'

'Just before the Nelligan show, yeah. That was our last conversation, I think.'

A drunken, anguished one from his side, if memory served…

'Yeah, so that's me. Oh, aside from, I gave up the flat in Cambridge so am currently of no fixed abode.'

'A Rolling Stone, in other words.'

He indulged Carl with a chuckle. 'Your patients must appreciate the Valentine comic touch.'

'Oh, they do.' There was a small pause, Carl drinking something. Probably tea. 'I have them in literal stitches.'

Carl!

Eternal master of the one-liner. But he needed to move them on now, answer Carl's last question because it was the most important…

'As to where I am, you're probably not going to believe this, but I'm on the Croatian island of Hvar right now, and yes, before you ask, I *have* seen Izzy.'

Silence.

'Carl?'

'I'm here. Just picking myself back up off the floor. *Geez!* What are the chances?' And then his tone shifted, instantly readable. 'When you say *seen*…?'

'I mean I've talked to her.'

'Ah! So I guess this call is partly redundant, then. You're already up to speed with the wedding that never was, Steady Eddie chucking my sister at the altar.'

'Yes.'

'How was she when you saw her? Mum tried calling her earlier, and so did I, but she didn't pick up. Maybe her phone is on silent if she's napping or maybe it's switched off, but it shouldn't be, because she's staying in this remote villa all by herself, and—'

'I know where she's staying, Carl. And don't worry. She's okay…'

Carl's breath hitched, then released. 'Thank God. Thanks, Finn…' There was another short pause to drink, a sense of Carl steadying himself. 'So, fill me in. If you know where she's staying, is that because she told you, or because you've been there, or what? Are the two of you hanging out?'

So many questions. Understandable! But where to begin?

He licked his lips. 'Okay, so the—'

'Because if you've got the time, I'd really appreciate it if you could keep an eye on her. Check in with her, you know. Just to be a friendly face. Why are you on Hvar, again?'

Again…?

As if he had told Carl already and Carl had forgotten.

A bad sign. Like talking across him. Carl was clearly stressing over Izzy, shouldering his mother's concern too, and who knew what else at work.

At least Finn was here. Could help. It would just be a case of—

'She was completely blindsided, Finn!'

He let go of his thought. Carl was shaping up to vent. Nothing for it but to listen.

'I mean *totally* floored. Everyone was. Probably me more than anyone, though, because I'm telling you, Finn, Eddie was *seriously* dull, you know what I'm saying?'

Not quite yet. But all the signs said he was about to find out, get chapter and verse about Eddie's failings. Shame on him that he was all ears, but how not to be interested when Carl had only ever made the odd oblique comment about Eddie in the past, and about Izzy? He had never coloured in the picture before.

'I mean, I couldn't believe the guy actually had it in him to go for high-stakes drama. Not that I was applauding or anything. Far from it.' Carl's tone downshifted. 'I'm not sorry it happened, though. For Izzy's sake, I'm sorry it happened *like* it did, but I'm not sorry. The way I see it, better late than never, because he wasn't right for her.'

Another pause, sipping, swallowing.

'She wouldn't hear it, though! Not from me, the lone dissenting voice. I took her aside at her engagement party, tried to tell her she was bonkers for tying herself down to her first and only ever boyfriend, especially *him*. I said she should at least *date* some other people, spread her wings a bit before she let Eddie put a ring on it, but no! She'd found her lobster, and I was just this massive killjoy raining on her precious parade.

'But I wasn't being a killjoy! Wasn't trying to rain on anything. I know Iz and I weren't close growing up, but I could just *feel* she was selling herself short with Eddie. I mean, don't get me wrong, he was good on paper. Decent-looking, smart enough, pleasant. Nice, you might say. And his family was well-heeled. But he didn't have two live sparks to rub together, not that I could see. He was boring. Not a catch. Not like you, Finn.'

What?

And then Carl was snickering. 'Do you remember how all the girls at school used to fall at your feet?'

Same ground he had already covered with Izzy. Clearly it wasn't for nothing that Carl and Izzy were twins…

'I was a flirt, that's why.'

'Yes, you were. Shameless! But you got away with it because you had it all going on, and I don't just mean the looks and the smarts and the drums. It's something deeper, vitality at the core of you, shining out. And before you think I'm about to propose to you, the point I'm trying to make is that I could always see the attraction with you, could see *why* a girl would fancy you. Hell, if I'd been a girl, *I'd* have fancied you. But Eddie? Blank space.'

So Eddie was a blank space, while he himself was a catch! Maybe it spoke to some character flaw in him that he was getting a happy kick out of that, feeling lighter inside suddenly, but there it was. No time to pick it apart, though. Carl wasn't talking, and so...

'Look, I'm really sorry about what's happened, Carl. To fill you in, though, put your mind and your mum's mind at rest, Izzy's place is barely a kilometre from where I'm staying. She has my number, so if she needs anything...'

'Thanks, Finn.' Carl's voice filled with a smile, and relief. 'I'm glad you're there. Mum and Dad will be too.' A brief silence followed. 'Why are you there, again?'

Seriously?

He permitted himself an eye roll. 'I'm here

with the band, recording our next album. We're working with a Croatian producer.'

'Nice! All that *warm Dalmatian sunshine.* Sounds like a really *tough* gig.'

Giving it all the emphasis.

Typical Carl!

'Leave off with the sarcasm. It *is* actually proving to be tough. The others are at war over how the album should sound.'

'Ah, right, so you'll be giving them a wide berth, then.'

He felt warmth flooding in. Such a nice feeling, being known by an old friend. Something to treasure, not let slip away…

He smiled. 'Yes, I am. Which means, in reference to your earlier question about keeping an eye on Izzy, I do have time to do that. As to how she is…' Perhaps simplest was best here, since Carl intended to call her anyway. 'She's going through it, obviously, but she's basically all right. I bumped into her in town this afternoon, left her eating ice cream at about quarter to five. She had a bag with her, so her phone was probably in there, and she just didn't hear it ringing. But she'll likely be home by now. I'm sure you'll get her if you try again.'

'Okay. Thanks.' Carl's voice cracked a little. 'I can't tell you what it means that you're there to look out for her, Finn. *You* out of all the people I know.'

His heart caught.

What to say...?

He forced himself to swallow. 'Thanks, but anyone would do the same.'

'I don't know about that.' Little pause. 'Anyway, it's been good to hear your voice. I won't leave it so long next time, and next time, we'll talk more about the band, I promise. I want to know everything you're up to. Take care, bud.'

'You too, Carl.'

And then he was gone.

Finn pulled in a breath and slipped his phone back into his pocket. So Carl wanted him to keep tabs on Izzy...

Not exactly a hardship!

As long as Izzy was okay with it. His heart dipped. And as long as he didn't go getting himself tangled up in her eyes, and in her smile, because nothing good could come of it. She wasn't in any position to take him on. As for himself, after today, God only knew what his position was.

Meanwhile, Jax was in the studio, probably drumming his fingers on the mixing desk by now, so taking himself apart to discover his position would have to wait until later, until they had somehow nailed this elusive twang of Jax's!

CHAPTER NINE

CARL'S VOICE CRACKED a little. 'Izzy, I really *am* sorry it happened like that...'

She gripped her phone hard, bearing down to hold back a tide of emotion. He was sorry about the *way* it happened, but he wasn't sorry that it *had* happened. Then again, why would he be? He had held his line about Eddie all these years, stuck to his guns. It was only fair to concede now, give him his due...

'You were right, though, Carl. About everything.'

Silence. And then...

'That doesn't make me happy.'

Scalding tears pricked her eyes. 'Do you think I don't know that?'

Because how could she not know it now? That all he had ever been trying to do was look out for her. It was totally in keeping in character. Because *that* was who Carl was, what he did every day of his life. He cared for people, healed people, looked after people. So why not her? Why not his own sister?

And what had she done? Flipped him off at her engagement party when it was the last thing he deserved, when she would have been better off listening to him. Maybe it was late in the day to be conceding, apologising, but it was important, only right. Particularly since he was calling to check in with her, full of concern and full of instructions about looking after herself and *not* burying her phone so deep in her bag that she couldn't hear it ringing. And also full of how amazing it was that Finn was here, how delighted he had been to call Finn for a catch-up and find *that* out! Full of how much better he felt about her being here alone now that Finn had agreed to keep an eye on her, because he was a diamond, a real stand-up guy.

As if she needed enlightening on that score!

But she couldn't think about Finn just now. She needed to keep this ball rolling, talk things out with Carl, start rebuilding the bridge she had broken so long ago…

'I'm sorry I reacted how I did when you tried to talk to me at our engagement party.'

He let out a short little breath. 'Well, I could have picked a choicer moment so, I'm also sorry.'

Taking half the blame. Making her eyes sting with tears again.

She swallowed hard. 'You've got nothing to be sorry for. I shouldn't have got so damn snarky!

In any case, the point is that whatever Eddie and I had together, it wasn't enough. You saw it and I didn't…' Her heart rolled. 'But I swear, when Eddie and I first got together, it *felt* like the real deal. He made me feel seen, Carl. Made me feel good. He made me feel like I counted. And it was so nice, feeling like that, seeing it in his eyes. It was elevating, and bolstering, and so, so special. I thought *that* feeling was love…'

'Oh, Izzy. You'd have been seen and then some, if you'd only ventured out into the light more, opened yourself up to people. I *tried* to tell you. If you'd put yourself out there more, you'd have had guys queuing up, found someone with a bit more va-va-voom.'

Like Finn…

But had he only sprung to mind because she was still wearing his shirt, could smell his lovely smell, feel his lovely shape in its folds? Because she was messed up and empty and he was balm for the soul, filling her senses, making them sit up straight for the first time in forever…

Carl's voice filtered in. 'That's all I ever wanted for you, Iz. Just for you to widen the playing field for yourself a bit before you got engaged.' He gave a little scoff. 'Ironic, isn't it? We were never close, and yet it's like I'm the *only* one who can see you. Maybe those nine months in the womb with you gave me a secret insight.'

'I think that only happens with identical twins.'

He chuckled. 'I know this, being a doctor and everything, but still, it's a captivating theory, isn't it? That while Mum and Dad were waxing lyrical, bathing in the sunshine streaming out of Eddie's backside, buddying up with Molly and Eddie Sr, I was like—*what*?'

She felt her lips curving. She could so picture Carl right now, bugging his eyes in that comic way he did.

'You're funny.' Her heart gave a little skip of recognition. 'I can see how you and Finn got on so well. He's funny too.'

Carl's chuckle deepened. 'He is. We used to crack each other up big time at school. We still do.' Then his laughter subsided. 'It would do you good to be around him, Izzy. He's super easy going, good company, an all-round—'

'*Stand-up guy.* I know.'

The kind to give up his shirt for a damsel in distress. But she wasn't telling Carl about *that*. She had filled him in about her various encounters with Finn, but only lightly, making them sound incidental, making herself sound casual, and not at all as though she was in a flat spin over him. But she was, with no let-up in sight since she'd *had* to text him about his shirt, and he had texted back saying that if it was okay, he would call round in the morning to collect it—all of that going on even before Carl had announced that he had tasked Finn with keeping an eye on her, multiplying the tailspin effect by the power of *oh my God what?*

'I'm *so* pleased he's close by, Iz.'

'I'm getting that…'

'No, but seriously. I can sleep easy now.' As if he had triggered himself, he let out a long, audible yawn. 'And talking of sleep, I should crash. I'm on early shift tomorrow.'

Her heart squeezed. Carl, always so hard at it, giving so much of himself to others.

She made her voice gentle. 'Go then. Sleep well. Thanks for checking in.'

'What else was I going to do? I worry about you, Izzy.' And then his tone switched to doctor mode. 'Now, remember. Eat well! Rest! Heal! And maybe *try* to have a holiday?' And with that he was gone.

She toyed with her phone.

A holiday…

Finn had said the same thing, hadn't he?

Could she get herself into that frame of mind?

She got up and walked to the edge of the terrace so she could see the beach below, tinted gold now in the lowering sun. She was definitely feeling lighter for having squared things away with Carl. And there was some Finn-related lightness going on too. Happy little beats skipping through her because he was coming by in the morning. Anticipation rippling through her, like before those school show rehearsals. The prospect of seeing him, getting to spend a whole hour in the same room as him.

A nice feeling.

A lovely, electric, alive feeling.

Her stomach dipped. But not a feeling she could let herself get hooked on or let factor into this business of cultivating a holiday mindset, because surely that mindset had to come from within, from some material change inside herself. It surely hinged on her, and her alone…

She touched Finn's shirt, then stripped it off. *Not helping!*

Finn was lovely. Good to be around. He was comforting. Amusing. She was never *not* going to smile at the thought of him, never not going to be pleased to see him, but this holiday mindset thing— it was down to her. Down to her, to put Eddie and everything that went with him onto the back burner, to clean her slate and freshen her outlook. Not the easiest thing to do when she couldn't quite wipe away that devastating moment at the altar, when the thought of it brought her down, but she had to try, try to find a fresh breeze beneath her wings and fly herself up. Up, up, and away. Flying solo!

CHAPTER TEN

'WHAT DO YOU THINK?' Izzy was biting her lip, looking at him keenly. 'Too strong? Too weak?'

Such intensity over a cup of espresso! Then again, coffee *was* a serious matter, so maybe he should curb his amusement before it showed and focus on the taste rather than on the barista.

'It's good.' He took another sip to be sure, holding it on his tongue before letting it slip down. 'Just right, I'd say.'

Her chin dipped. 'You're not just being nice?'

What?

'No! I'm not *that* nice! But what's the big deal, anyway? Why are you looking so worried?'

Her face tightened. 'I'm not looking worried.'

He shook his head, then switched to nodding to make her smile. 'Okay, if you say so.'

Her cheeks dimpled for a satisfying moment, but then her expression reverted to serious. 'The big deal is that I've never made espresso before, never used one of those pot things, but you're an expert, and that's a *lot* of pressure.'

Pressure?

Nothing to do with him! He hadn't asked her to make coffee, hadn't even asked to come in. He had only come here to pick up his shirt and check in, as per Carl's request, had determined beforehand that he would leave straight after, to prove to himself that he could rise above Carl's words yesterday and *not* use them to give himself licence to hang out with Izzy, making a nuisance of himself. Which plan would also have spared him desire, temptation, and all the soul searching and internal angst that went with those things, had it worked. Had he come armed with a coping strategy for Izzy opening the door in a T-shirt and cut-offs, smiling into his eyes for what felt like an eternity, before finally announcing that she had made coffee and would he like some?

But he hadn't armed himself. So, now, here he was, stuck, charmed, perplexed and suddenly desperate to say the right thing. Because while there was a faintly wry light in her eyes, something behind her gaze spoke to that inexplicable insecurity of hers too, and he couldn't bear to see it, wanted to shoo it away.

'It's coffee, Iz. Not life or death.'

She blinked.

'But it *is* good.' He smiled to warm her. 'You did a good job. And lots of people don't know how to make espresso, so it's not like a character failing or anything. It's all pods now, isn't it? Or French press.'

Her expression softened. 'That's true. I just thought I'd give it a go, you know, since there was some coffee left from yesterday.' Little sigh. 'Just to flex different muscles…' She frowned. 'There are so many things I haven't done, Finn. *Tried.* I know making espresso isn't much, but it's a start.'

Such earnestness!

He smiled. 'Today espresso, tomorrow the world!'

She chuckled. 'I wouldn't go that far, but sort of.' Then her eyes came fully to his. 'Both you and Carl have said to me that I should *try* to have a holiday. And last night, I was thinking about that, about how as well as being relaxing, a holiday should be about trying new things, experiencing new things…'

They had talked about Carl as they had come out here to sit, Izzy pressing him on exactly what he had told Carl about her tabletop antics in the bar. He'd reassured her that he hadn't said a word, had kept things general.

No need to explain that he had his own reasons for that. And no need to mention all the bolstering things Carl had said to him either, since, whilst it had been a buzz to hear them, had temporarily set his heart alight with possibilities, it had come to him pretty quickly afterwards that what Carl thought about him didn't change a thing. It didn't change his reality, or Izzy's…

He might be free right now, languishing, but most of the time he was on the go, in constant motion. Life was crazy. Chaotic! He wasn't boyfriend material. Assuming Izzy would even be interested in him. And how to judge that? For sure, it had felt like she was flirting with him yesterday, but the line between 'flirting and fun was hellish narrow. And the odds were well against him. She was down one devastating break-up, after all, had more than a decade's worth of history with Eddie to get over, a home to dismantle. She wouldn't be rising from those ashes anytime soon, no matter how good she got at trying new things. Speaking of which…

'So, what have you got in mind? Hang-gliding? Bungee jumping?'

'No chance!' Shaking her head. 'I'm not *that* adventurous.'

'Who's to say? You might well be. Trouble is, you only find that stuff out if you take the leap, and if you hate it…' He gripped his cheeks, mimicking Munch's *The Scream* to make her laugh, which she did, roundly, *gratifyingly*!

Then she was gathering herself again, her eyes

fastening on his. 'So what's the scariest thing *you've* ever done?'

He felt a skip inside. Seriously, she was handing him *this* on a plate?

Too delicious!

He looked skywards, pretending to ponder. 'Erm… I think, maybe, possibly, drinking that espresso you just made.'

Her face stretched. 'Finn Falco! You're a horror. I hate you!'

And yet it felt so damned good.

He grinned. 'No, you don't. I gave you the shirt off my back, remember? You can't hate a person who does that.'

Staring at him, and then suddenly her face broke apart, and she was laughing, her eyes full of bewitching, sparkling light. 'Okay, I don't hate you, but it could come to that if you don't watch your step.'

'Noted…'

His heart stilled. And if he didn't watch it, he was going to get himself tangled up in all this lovely back-and-forth. Get himself lost in her eyes, and her smile, yearning for the impossible. Which meant he should leave right now, before the longing became a torment. Or worse, led him into doing something he would only regret.

He drew up a smile, flattening his palms on

the table to signal his imminent departure. 'So what are your plans for the day?'

Her eyes clocked his hands then jumped to his. 'I'm going to go down to my little beach. Have a swim and a sunbathe.'

'Nice…' Going down those wonky stone steps to the rough descending path that disappeared enticingly through the trees. Presumably it led all the way to that pretty little cove he had stood admiring yesterday while he had been waiting for her to reappear for—

'Yes.' Her voice pulled him back. 'I think *that* probably *is* the way down…'

That being the corner of the terrace he hadn't noticed his eyes wandering off to. But what about that other word she had used?

He looked at her. '*Probably?* You mean you don't know, haven't been down yet?'

She shook her head. 'No. Today will be my first time.' And then she smiled, rounding her eyes into his. 'A whole *new* experience!'

Adorable!

But thinking that wasn't helping him, and neither was lingering.

He got to his feet. 'Look at you, racking up the new experiences already.'

'Yeah. I'm totally smashing it…' She caught her lip between her teeth, seeming to drift for a moment, and then her eyes refocused, locking on to his softly. 'Would you like to come and experience it with me?'

His heart broke its chains.

Did he ever, *all day long*, want to go with her!

Gorgeous beach. Gorgeous water. Gorgeous Izzy.

Izzy in a swimsuit...

More lovely back-and-forth banter. More teasing her, watching that smile rising in her, taking over her lovely face. More tingling happiness inside him that he was the one who could brighten her like that, the one making it happen, the one bathing in the light of that smile.

His stomach caught. But going would cost him too, increase this longing, this torment. As for his heart...

Grounds enough to decline, make out he had other plans.

Except...

How would it feel for Izzy to be sitting down there all by herself?

Lonely? Sad? Miserable?

His heart clenched. Didn't bear thinking about.

Oh God! And what about safety? What if she got a cramp swimming? Or her foot got stuck in a crevice in the rocks with the tide coming in? Or what if a stranger rocked up? A weirdo. A guy. A weirdo-guy! For sure, it was a private beach, but who knew?

So many dangers lurking.

Not a risk he could take, letting her go alone, especially this first time. And Carl would agree. Carl would definitely want him to go. So there it was.

He reconnected with her gaze and smiled. 'Sure, I'll come with you. I'm always up for a new experience!'

CHAPTER ELEVEN

'I CAN'T BELIEVE you haven't been down here before, Iz.'

She bit the inside of her cheek. If Finn was struggling to believe *that*, then he should have been in her shoes, because *she* couldn't believe that he was walking along the narrow path behind her at her behest, that she had actually *invited* him to come with her.

So much for solo flying!

How had she deviated from her plan so quickly? Caved! It was only supposed to have been coffee. A convivial coffee together because Finn was a friend now, good company, someone she wanted to spend a bit of time with. Plus, he was qualified in espresso, so had been the perfect guinea pig for her first espresso rodeo. But she had meant for it to end there, for Finn to go off and do his thing while she did hers. Separate ways. Nice, safe, unconfusing, very separate ways.

Best laid plans.

Out. The. Window.

Weakness! Her new middle name. Her heart paused. Or maybe not new at all, not when it came to Finn…

If only he hadn't made her laugh so much with his *Scream* face, or got her with that drinking-the-espresso-she'd-made-was-the-scariest-thing-he'd-ever-done gag… If only he hadn't been looking so handsome in his jeans and pale linen shirt, shades perched on his head, thumb ring glinting… If only being with him hadn't been feeling so good… If only the thought of sitting on the beach by herself hadn't suddenly conjured up the word *depressing* rather than *intrepid… If only, if only, if only…* Then maybe she would have been able to ignore the way he had lit up and glanced toward the steps when she had mentioned the beach, and she wouldn't have folded like paper. But there it was.

So here they were now, going down the dirt path through a tunnel of trees, glinting sunshine above them, tantalising glimmers of sparkling turquoise sea ahead, breathing in pine resin and the warm, dry breath of earth, and it was so, so, beautiful.

Magical!

And literally on her doorstep.

No wonder Finn couldn't believe it was her first time!

She glanced back to catch his eye, going for an upbeat tone to offset the misery of remembering. 'I know. Epic fail not to have ventured down yet, right? But it *was* nighttime when I first arrived, and I *was* somewhat the worse for too many double vodkas on the plane—drowning my sorrows, wouldn't you know—so exploring wasn't a priority. Then, when I woke up and remembered everything, all I wanted to do was blot it out, so I hit the fridge, got going with the so-called celebration champagne—'

'You were on a bender, in other words.'

'I suppose so. Two days straight drinking, sleeping and online shopping—'

'For a sparkly dress and shoes?'

Her heart flinched. 'Yes, but please don't judge me.' Because the thought of that, on top of the guilt she was already feeling, was too much. 'I was angry. Bitter. I wanted to put the boot in, make Eddie pay, but I'm going to pay it back, all of—'

'Your business, not mine, Izzy.' His hand touched her shoulder briefly from behind. 'I *wasn't* judging you.'

A relief. Making her eyes prickle with tears. And maybe she would need to think about the whys of that later, but right now there was just the challenge of containing it, slanting her tone back toward lightness.

'I'm glad, because that person wasn't me.' And for what it was worth… 'Also, that crazy drunken dancing chick in the bar wasn't me either.'

'Aw, damn! You mean you can't dance?'

She felt her insides kinking. Oh, how did he do that? Crack a smile out of her so easily.

She glanced back. 'Very funny!'

'What do you mean?'

Playing dumb. Enjoying it, too, if the amusement in his voice was anything to go by.

She spun round to fire him the expected look, only just managing not to catch her breath at the sight of him, at the warm flash of his gaze. 'I'm going to ignore that and get back to the point, which is because of all the bender stuff, and because I booked a spa session in town, et cetera, et cetera, et cetera, I simply haven't had a chance to come down here yet.'

He set his smiling lips. 'Fair enough.' Then he was tipping his head back, looking up into the trees. 'It's really something, though, isn't it? So peaceful. Just lovely…'

'Yes, it is.'

Her heart rippled.

Like you.

And maybe letting herself think it was a weakness, but how could she not think it when it was so blindingly true? Finn *was* lovely. A lovely soul. Lovely to be with. Carl thought so, and why shouldn't she? Seeing it didn't mean she had actual designs on him.

As if!

As if she had the appetite for another mistake. As if she even had a scrap of heart left to make a mistake with. No! She was simply glad that Finn was here. Glad of his company, and his friendship, and if he was happy, then…

Her heart paused. Was he happy, though? Looking up into the trees, pack hanging off his shoulder, he seemed content, but was he genuinely okay about this, about coming with her?

She turned, walking on. Because who knew with Finn? He was so good-natured… Pulling swim shorts from his pack to show her, shorts he always had with him on his travels around the island, he said, because he loved the water and liked to stop for a swim. Beach ready!

But he had been all set to leave before she had mentioned coming down here, hadn't he? Hands pressed to the table. That restless edge about him, as if he had plans. And yes, his eyes *had* sparked when she had mentioned the beach, but what if that hadn't been interest as such? It could just as easily have been simple recognition, because he had clocked the steps the other day and was putting two and two together. Steps and beach! Steps *to* path *to* beach!

Oh God!

What if the only reason he had said yes was that he had felt put on the spot, felt that he couldn't say no? There was the Carl factor, too, Carl asking him to keep an eye on her. That would carry some weight with him. There *had* been that long deliberating second straight after she had asked him, after all, his gaze flickering, busy weighing things up.

And now it was in her head, she was only going to stew if she didn't check in with him, give him a chance to duck out, because he didn't deserve to be feeling put-upon, press-ganged. Not after all his kindness.

She anchored her tote strap on her shoulder and turned. 'Finn?'

His eyes found hers. 'Izzy?'

'Can I just check? Are you really okay with this?'

'Define *this*.'

'Coming to the beach with me.'

He recoiled ever so slightly. 'Of course I am. Why?' Then he was coming toward her, his gaze raking over her face. 'Are you okay? What's brought this on?'

A foolish notion, patently. And now she was trapped in a hole of her own making, one she was going to have to dig herself out of fast.

'Nothing.' She smiled and shook her head,

rolling her eyes to seem light and ditzy. 'Just a glitch in the matrix. Forget it.' She turned to walk. 'Let's—'

'No.' His hand caught her arm gently from behind, and a second later he was in front of her again, shaking his head. 'I can't forget it, because you must have said it for a reason.' He settled his shoulders as if he was staging a sit-in. 'Tell me.'

Perfect!

Finn was blessed with a stubborn streak.

She pulled in a breath. 'Okay, fine. I just had a sudden thought that maybe you'd felt obliged to come.'

His brows went up. 'Why on earth would you think that?'

Oh Lordy!

'Because you were setting yourself up to leave until I asked you, as though you had plans. And because you're nice. You probably thought that I'd make a sad prospect sitting down here on my own, so maybe felt you couldn't say no. And I know that Carl's asked you to keep an eye on me, so there's that as well.'

'Wow!' His jaw flexed. 'Okay, so you're only about ninety-eight percent wide of the mark.'

'Which means I'm two percent right.'

He gave a wry smile. 'And that's the hill you want to die on?'

'If it's all I've got.'

'Fine.' He let out a sigh. 'Carl *did* cross my mind, yes, but only because I was thinking about safety—you getting a cramp or slipping on the rocks or something. I thought if *I* was thinking it, then Carl would be too, that he wouldn't want me to let you come down here by yourself.' Shrugging. 'But before that, all I'd been thinking was, great, beach trip!'

Which, come to think of it, she *had* caught in his eyes before all the other stuff set in, making the moment feel endless. Stuff about safety, not remotely about feeling put-upon.

Ninety-eight percent wide of the mark!

Reassuring, but also a smidge embarrassing.

She forced a swallow, willing her cheeks not to flush. 'Okay, well, thanks for clearing that up.' She found a smile and aimed it at him. 'I confess *I* didn't think about the safety aspect. Kudos on that.'

The corners of his mouth twitched up. 'Cheers, but I don't want kudos. I want to know if you've ever heard of Occam's razor.'

What?

Was he pranking her now? That light in his eyes… Always so hard to tell.

She shook her head. 'No. What is it? Some scary sea thing, a stingy razor clam thingy?'

'No.' Chuckling. 'It's not marine life. It's a

philosophical principle. Simply put, it states that if there are several possible explanations for something, the simplest, most obvious one is likeliest to be correct.' Dipping his chin now, holding her gaze keenly, waiting for some penny to drop with her, it felt like. But she couldn't feel anything coming, couldn't seem to think past this sudden uneasy swirling sensation inside her.

She licked her lips quickly. 'Okay, and you're telling me this why?'

A ripple moved through his gaze. 'I suppose I'm trying to say, in a very gentle way, that you need to stop overthinking things. I'm saying that I'm here because I want to be.' A smile ghosted over his lips. 'I'm saying you need to have a little faith, Iz.'

What?

Her blood lit.

Faith!

He dared to lecture her, of all people, about faith! Was he actually *trying* to trigger her?

She snatched up a breath. 'Thanks for the advice, Finn, but strangely enough, I've got a bit of a problem with faith right now...' And also, suddenly, a problem with looking at him, because the stung look in his eyes was freshening her pain somehow, drawing tears and fury up through her, and she couldn't bear it.

She broke away, walking fast, spewing it

out, all the bitter spit and crackle, for the sheer, heavenly release of it. '*Curiously enough*, getting jilted does that to you, you know? Shreds your faith—no! Kills it dead. You start to question everything, and everyone, but mostly you question yourself, because guess what? That's who you're left with in the end. Your own stupid self. Your failings. Your mistakes. Everything that's wrong with you that got you falling for the wrong person and paying the price! Everything that's wrong with you that kept you blind to what was *so obviously* coming down the tracks sooner or later. Everything you believed in, every damn thing about yourself. And the next minute, there you are, so down on yourself, so full of misery and self-doubt, that you're looking under rocks for reasons anyone could possibly, genuinely, want to go to the damn beach with you—'

'You think I don't know that?' Finn was beside her now. And then he was in front of her, blocking her way, filling her gaze with the blaze in his. 'Please credit me with some vision. Some *understanding...*' He flexed his jaw. 'Do you honestly think I can't see where you're at, Izzy? *Do* you?' He swallowed. 'I was trying to nudge you out of that headspace for the exact reason that I *can* see it, but I absolutely wasn't criticising you or judging you.' Shaking his head now. '*Of course* you're out of faith after what you've been through. *Of course* you're running the gamut. I'd expect nothing less…' His gaze flashed away, then came back, fully loaded. 'I'd expect nothing less because I *get* what you're going through. And I *get* what you're going through because I've been there, done it, got the T-shirt.' His shoulders rose on a heaving breath. Then he was closing his eyes, talking on. 'Just before the band broke into the big time, *literally* three days before we did that TV show, I was dumped. Not at the altar, granted, and with hindsight, not wholly unforeseeable. But like you, in the moment that it came, it threw me for a loop, so, you know…' His eyes opened, his gaze focusing on hers. 'Same effect.'

Same anguish. Same pain. Same hurt. All there, moving behind his eyes.

She felt her heart crumbling, hot tears trying to escape. Did this honey of a man have a single selfish bone in his body? Showing her his pain to help her with her own. Opening up so she wouldn't feel like the only freak in the room. *Yet again*, doing right by her. *Yet again*, stopping her in her tracks, leaving her astonished and humbled searching for breath to speak with.

'I'm so sorry, Finn.' She put her hand on his arm, because how could she not touch him now, not want to convey more than she could say with words?

He shook his head a little. 'No need to be. And no need to—' His gaze shifted momentarily, taking in the wetness she could feel at the edges of her eyes. 'I just couldn't have you thinking I was coming at this blind.'

Because blind wouldn't have cut it with her, would it? Wouldn't have pulled her up short, jumped her out of her own head so swiftly, so high was she on grief—grief for all the time she had wasted, chances she had missed—so bent on lashing out, striding off, losing it.

Not her finest hour.

And now she needed to own it, apologise.

She took her hand back. 'I'm sorry for blowing up at you like that. It just happened, boiled up out of nowhere. I didn't mean to—'

'I know that.' Cutting in, kindness in his eyes. 'You don't need to apologise.'

Because he understood. Because he had been there, done it, got the T-shirt. Because he wasn't flying blind.

But she was. Because what did she know about his love life, aside from his uni one-night stand? She felt a flutter. Then again, now that he had opened a door, wouldn't this be the perfect moment to change that? To ask? Not to pry, but to be a support, to lend him a sympathetic ear. She felt a rise in her chest, a sudden small rush of warmth. Surely this was her chance to stop thinking about herself and focus on Finn, step up and be a friend to him.

She let the thought into her gaze, let it shape her smile. 'Well, it helps to know you've been through something similar, that you get it.'

His lips moved toward a smile but then suddenly he was frowning instead, pressing two fingers to his eyebrow. 'To be honest, now that I think about it, it's probably not that similar, aside from the shock factor and the immediate devastation, but if it helps…' He gave a light shrug then turned his gaze along the path. 'Shall we push on before the sea runs dry?'

Before she started asking him questions, more like!

Her pulse double-skipped. Or was she overthinking things again, imagining that he didn't want to talk, when in fact he simply wanted to get to the beach?

Only one way to find out…

She switched her tote to her other shoulder. 'Sure, let's go.'

At least they could walk side by side now that the path was wider.

Walking and talking.

Always easier.

She looked over. 'So, do you want to talk about it? About what happened with…?'

His eyes glanced into hers. 'Janine.'

'Janine. Right…'

She held her breath, but he didn't offer anything further, just kept on walking, looking ahead.

Was he still hurting too much to talk?

Her heart squeezed. The thought of it. That he was hurting, holding it inside, when she was here, ready to help. She couldn't not try again.

'I mean, it's only fair. You've listened to me enough, so if you want to offload to me—'

He scoffed. 'I think you've got more than enough on your plate already without listening to my woes.'

So stubborn!

'But what if I *want* to listen? What if I want to be there for you like you've been there for me?' She raised a brow. 'And not to be glib or anything, but in town yesterday, you were all for the power of distraction. Your woes could be a distraction from mine.'

'I was talking about cheerier distractions, Izzy.' His gaze pinned her for a beat, then moved on. 'Ice cream and sight-seeing, fun and sunshine, holiday stuff.'

In other words, *don't push it.*

Why, though? Why go so far, then retreat?

She chewed her lip. *His* business. And *hers* to respect. She pulled in a breath. Maybe that was fine. Being a friend wasn't about pushing, was it? It was about being there when you were needed, being there at just the right moment.

Her breath caught. And this moment definitely wasn't *that*, not with the path opening out now to this glorious white beach with its cluster of boulders at the far end, and all that glittering turquoise sea right there.

'Wow!' Finn drew up, breaking into his beautiful, easy smile. 'Now *this* is what I'm talking about! *This* is your distraction right here, Iz…'

And not a second too soon, because rebuffing her kind overtures, stonewalling to keep her at arm's length was painful, went against every one of his instincts.

But what else could he do? He had gone with his instincts earlier, hadn't he? Let himself feel her anguish in his own chest when she had launched into her downward spiral, only to find himself chasing down the path after her, desperate for her to know that he could see what she was going through, understood it—how it felt to be hurt, blindsided, left for dead.

All that fervour, springing from a well he didn't even know ran that deep, his heart beating for her right there on his sleeve: boom, boom, boom!

And he couldn't let it do that again, couldn't let himself do anything that would make it beat harder and louder, such as opening up to her about Janine. Because letting all of his pain out, and all of Izzy's warmth in, would only make him more vulnerable, even more susceptible to her than he was already, more likely to slide over a fatal edge, and for countless reasons, he couldn't take that risk. Not with Izzy…

Izzy, who was turning to look at him now with no trace of what had just passed in her eyes, only a warm, beautiful, breaking smile.

'You're right. *This* is a proper distraction.' Then she laughed, turning to look at it again. 'I can't believe I've got my own private little beach!'

He felt a smile loosening. Such delight in her! So good to see after all that earlier browbeating and bitterness. It was setting his heart to rights, bringing ease back, lightness…

'Well, you have, so you're just going to have to learn to live with it.'

She caught her lip in her teeth. 'I don't think that'll be a stretch.'

Which was what she deserved after everything she'd been through. To be *not* stretched, or bent out of shape, but just to be at one with herself, at one in her space. And on that beat…

'Where do you want to set up camp?'

She made a quick scan. 'What about by that

nice flat boulder in the middle?' Her eyes locked on his, sparking mischief. 'Race you?'

Torch to a flame! Inner child loading.

He grinned. 'Okay, you're on.'

'We'll do one-two-three, yeah?'

Cosi adorabile!

'It's your party, your beach.'

Laughing. 'So it is…' And then she was bending forward, gripping her bag, looking over. 'Okay. On one…two…three!'

He launched, and in the same beat, Izzy yelped.

Oh no!

He felt his heart sinking. How could he have forgotten to warn her?

He turned back, guilt warming his cheeks at the sight of her rigid figure. 'I'm sorry, Iz. I should have said. It's marble grit, brutal on the feet. It's why they sell those aqua shoe thingies everywhere.'

She lifted a pained gaze to his. 'Oh, right. So *that* explains it!'

What to say?

'Your sandals will be trapping it, making it worse. You might be better going barefoot.'

Her gaze solidified. 'Says the man wearing biker boots!'

Fair point.

'Well, yes. Sorry.'

She shifted a little, wincing. 'Stop saying sorry. It's not your fault.' And then she was sitting herself down, stripping off her sandals, shoving them into her tote. 'Hand up, please?'

He obliged.

'Okay...' Testing her feet. 'It still hurts, but not as much.' Her eyes came to his. 'What are you doing, still standing there in your boots?'

That gaze on her, full of challenge...

'I see.' He felt a smile coming. 'So the race is still on?'

'Of course!' Her brows went up. 'But if I'm limping, then so are you. Even playing field, right?'

'Absolutely...' He dropped down, shedding his boots and socks, holding on to a chuckle. Probably best not to mention that he had been walking these beaches for a couple of weeks now, had it down to a fine art.

Why spoil the fun?

He turned up his jeans so they wouldn't impede, then got to his feet. 'Right. I'm ready.'

'Okay.' She flashed a smile, then braced, her eyes merry on his. 'On one...two...three!'

He launched, taking long strides for speed, going for the flat dips, avoiding the mounds that sank the second you put weight on them, and then he was there, dropping his stuff on the boulder, feeling a stupid victorious rush of pure unadulterated glee. 'I won!'

'Oh, bully for you!'

He turned, felt laughter erupting in his chest. She was ten paces back, wincing and jerking her way toward him, arms out like she was walking a tightrope, her face screwed tight as a ball.

How could he resist teasing her?

'That didn't sound very heartfelt, Iz.'

She wagged her head. 'Meh, meh, meh, meh, meh…not very heartfelt…look at *me*. I won. I'm the best! Meh, meh, meh, meh, meh.'

So funny!

'Nice! Very mature.' *Perhaps a little encouragement…* 'Come on, Iz. Chop-chop!'

Her eyes snapped up, sending him the death stare. 'I'll give you chop-chop in a minute.'

His heart leapt. She would keep feeding him these irresistible cues…

He parked himself on the boulder, folding his arms for effect. 'Better make that ten minutes, the rate you're going.'

'Oh, you think you're so hilarious, don't you?' She chuckled down at the beach and shook her head. Then she looked up, giving him that fearsome mock scowl he loved. 'You just keep on going like that if you want to earn yourself some hefty retribution.'

Oh, this just got better and better…

He smiled into her eyes. 'See, the thing is, though, you'd actually have to catch me first, and, well…' He scratched his head to tease her. 'Need I say more?'

She winced another two steps, then looked up again, smiling sweetly. 'There's more than one way to skin a cat, Finn Falco. You might want to remember that…'

As if he could remember anything when she was looking at him like this, hair blowing, eyes full of magic. When she was looking so perfect in her T-shirt and cut-offs. When all he could think was that he wanted to go over, sweep her up into his arms, and kiss her…

His heart clenched.

Impossible!

Not a thought he should even be having, and the very reason he couldn't fully open up to her about Janine. Because if he did open up and let her in, then this connection he could already feel with her would only deepen, and these thoughts would come at him harder and faster, make it even more difficult for him *not* to make a move on her. And he couldn't risk that, put her in that position, because she was patently in no state to handle him, to start anything with him. Out of faith. Emotionally shredded. Trailing over a decade's worth of baggage. She didn't know where the hell she was at, or what she wanted, but she definitely wouldn't want anything he could offer her. More upside-down chaos than she had already got, a whirlwind life he was still trying to get a handle on himself. Not even a place of his own he could take her back to...

His heart shifted. And that wasn't even factoring in his own scars, his own issues with faith after Janine, which weren't exactly minor ones.

How would they come to manifest? Would he find himself doubting more and trusting less, find himself holding part of himself back all the time?

Who knew?

For that reason and all the other ones, *this*, right here, was the sum total of what he and Izzy could ever be. Friends. Flirty friends at a push. Teasing friends, definitely...one of whom was sitting here contemplating his own navel when it was his overdue turn to bat!

He refocused quickly, felt a familiar line rising together with a smile. 'Should I be afraid?'

Her eyes sparked with instant, fiendish recognition. 'Oh yes! If I were you, Finn, I'd be *very* afraid...'

CHAPTER TWELVE

Finn ran both hands over his head, smoothing back the dark, wet tangle of his hair. 'It's amazing, seeing Paradise Villa from here, don't you think, Iz?'

Back, turned. Droplets, beading on those nice shoulders of his. Gaze, usefully focused on the view. Could this be her moment to slip beneath the waves? She felt a delectable scheming flutter in her belly. It might be her only chance…

'Yeah, it is.' She lifted her chin, smiling to make her voice seem engaged and not at all as if she was bent on imminent retribution. 'It's cool, seeing everything from out here.'

Finn was pointing now. 'See how it sits on that little spur, the way the trees wrap round? You can really see how…'

She inhaled and dropped under, turning tail to dive down, deep enough that he wouldn't see her. Then she stopped, looking up toward the surface. *There!*

Treading water with his big, tough feet. Nice,

satisfying circles. Going round and round, looking for her no doubt, hopefully in a blind panic.

She smiled. Served him right for all that heckling and teasing earlier!

She moved in, waiting for his feet to slow, then clamped his ankles and tugged, kicking her legs fast to draw him down. Down and down and down in a flail of arms and bubbles and billowing hair, laughter bubbles streaming from his nose and mouth, and from her own. But then her lungs rebelled. She let him go, striking for the surface, felt him rising with her.

Two seconds later they were cresting, splashing and gasping, Finn, laughing into her eyes, flicking his head to shake off water.

'You're a bad girl, Izzy.'

Which somehow felt like a good thing. Powerful. Or maybe it was the light in his eyes that was making it feel that way. Regardless, she liked the feeling, the way it was drawing a smile up through her…

'You mean to tell me you didn't enjoy your just desserts?'

His brow crimped. '*Enjoy* isn't the word I'd have used. And neither is *just*.'

Seriously?

'You're contesting your punishment?'

'You're damned right I am, because no crime was committed.'

She felt an inside smile unwinding. Oh, the deliciousness of this exchange, little sparks jumping between them, the sublime electric thrill of it, like with the pepper mill. Impossible not lean into it, go with the flow. Impossible not to want to keep the flow going.

She drilled her gaze into his. 'How can you say that? You heckled me all the way to the boulder.'

'*Encouraged* you, Izzy.'

Teasing her with his eyes, setting off more delicious tingles inside her.

'It was one hundred percent heckling.' She tried to scowl. 'And you were laughing at me too.'

'Again, not a crime.'

'By what measure?'

He broke into an irresistible grin. 'By the measure of logic. You were funny to watch, so I laughed—all that *ooh*ing and *ouch*ing coming over to the boulder, more of the same when you were getting out of your shorts.' His smile widened, becoming a chuckle. 'As for when you were getting into the water and the beach shelved away, I'd argue it would have been a crime *not* to laugh…'

That moment of stepping into nothing, sinking to mid-thigh inside of a second, shrieking with shock, Finn hooting with laughter from his happy floating position.

She pressed her lips together to stop a smile slipping out. 'You're a menace.'

He wiped a hand over his face. 'You got me good, though, I admit. There I was, raving about the view, expecting you to reply, and suddenly you weren't there.' Something gave in his gaze. 'I confess I did panic a bit.'

Sorry, not sorry!

She pouted her lips to tease him. 'Aww. Poor Finn. Did you think I was lost at sea? Did you think I'd drowned?'

Shaking his head, frowning. 'No, not *drowned…*' He ran a tongue across his lip, his gaze solemn. 'I was actually worrying about the sharks.'

Her blood froze.

Sharks!

She drew her knees up, scanning the water. He was wrong, surely. There couldn't be sharks here. The villa brochure would have said so. Flagged it up. Great big letters! Great big—

Her heart lurched.

Total idiot, Izzy!

She looked up, and instantly Finn's face split. Then he was laughing, throwing his head back, shoulders shaking. 'Your face, Izzy!' Sculling backward a little, meeting her gaze again, his eyes glistening with gleeful tears. 'I'm sorry. I just couldn't resist.'

Couldn't resist teasing her. Couldn't resist beaming magical light into her eyes at every turn, giving her tingles, giving her his time and his attention like a devoted friend, making her feel cared about in a way that Eddie hadn't in a long, long time.

But what did any of it count for if he wouldn't open himself up, let her in properly, let her be a full and proper friend back to—

Don't, Izzy!

His business, not hers. *His* prerogative.

And not something to be thinking about when he was right here, smirking at her, all pleased with himself for reeling her in.

She hurled some water at his face to release a valve. 'I hate you, Finn Falco.'

Chuckling. 'No, you don't.'

'I do so!' And to make sure the last word was hers, she broke away, striking for the shore. But in seconds, he was there, front-crawling along beside her, probably thinking that this was another race because that was what they had been doing this past while, racing each other. Front crawl. Back crawl. Breaststroke. One lame, laughing attempt apiece at the butterfly. Racing back and forth, in between messing about. Finn doing handstands. Letting her stand on his shoulders so she could dive. Beckoning her to come stand still with him so the fish would come around their legs, his down-turned face rapt, his eyes shining like a kid's. He looked like the boy he must have been during those summers in Ireland, discovering his love for the great outdoors, darting glances into her eyes every so often. Dark amber glances flecked with gold.

Devastating.

Her heart fell. Not unlike the devasting effect that walking the ten steps back to their spot was going to have on her poor feet! Even worse, Finn was already there, towelling himself off, his gaze turning in her direction, lighting up, his whole divine body radiating mischief.

'Ah, Venus emerges...'

She fired him the expected look. 'Don't say another word, armour-feet!'

He let out a hoot of laughter. 'I've been called some things in my time, but that's a new one!'

She gritted her teeth, taking a few quick wincing steps while he was busy chuckling. 'I've got some others if you're interested.'

'Excellent.'

Another two torturous steps. 'Teflon toes.'

Towelling his hair now. 'Nice alliteration.'

Nice-hot-body-on-you-to-die-for...

She shook herself. *Maybe not!* And then, thankfully, she was stepping onto her beach mat. Nothing short of heavenly after the beach!

'Here...' Finn bent to pick up her towel, handing it over with a smile. 'You didn't yelp once this time. You must be acclimatising.'

'Or maybe I just didn't want you teasing me again!' She wrapped herself up quickly to keep his gaze on the straight and narrow, then aimed a smile into his eyes. 'Because that also works. Thanks for the towel, by the way.'

'You're welcome. And consider me told…' He drew a hand across his face like a curtain, his expression in its wake deadly solemn. 'No more teasing.'

If only his eyes weren't harbouring a twinkle in their depths, tickling her funny bone.

She dropped down onto her mat, stretching her legs out. 'Yeah, yeah. Like you're going to be able to keep that up for more than a minute.'

He laughed. 'You're probably right.' He spread his towel out, then sat down, hooking his arms around his knees. 'I'm "incorrigible", apparently.'

'Your mother's expression?'

He flashed a dimple. 'You catch on quick.'

'Hardly! It took me five whole seconds to spot that you were winding me up about sharks.' Her heart pinched out of nowhere. 'And let me see, a whole thirteen years to *not* spot that what Eddie and I had wasn't the real deal, wasn't—'

'Don't, Iz…' Cutting in, narrowing his gaze on hers. 'Don't go down that path now…'

Concern on his face, in his eyes. *Affinity.* Not wanting her to spiral downward, take the path least trodden. But not taking it, leaving it all grown over and undisturbed, wouldn't help her to understand, to process. And holding Finn's gaze like this wasn't helping anything at all. Not her heart rate, which was climbing. And most definitely not her hungry peripheral eye, which was taking in the shape of him, the curving swell of his shoulders and bicep muscles, his honed pecs and abs, the smattering of dark hair on his chest and that dusky trail…

She broke free, focusing on the incoming waves instead, the rolling break, the lacy spreading froth. 'Don't worry. I'm not going to lose it again. I'm just stunned at myself, at the two of us, how we could have gone on like that for so long.'

'Maybe there's nothing to be stunned about. You were obviously happy together for a long time.'

That word, *obviously*…

She couldn't not look over. 'You're invoking Occam's razor again?'

'Why not?' He gave a little shrug. 'You can bend your brain sifting through minutiae, or you can go with the obvious—that the two of you fell deeply in love, got engaged, were tight for a long time, but then your tank ran dry. It happens.'

And now that word, *deeply*…

'You make it sound so linear. So simple.' And not at all like the version that was nagging at her, the version where she had never really loved Eddie, only convinced herself that she did because of how he had made her feel. Taller. Better. More confident. The version where the tingles she had felt inside when he looked at her with those adoring, twinkling blue eyes of his weren't in her heart at all, but in her head. Ego tingles! She, Izzy, loving not him but being his number one. That feeling of being somebody's number one...

Or maybe she *was* overthinking it, just digging stupid rabbit holes for her mind to run down. *Whatever!* This endless self-examination was exactly what she had been ranting to Finn about earlier, what the whole wedding fiasco had brought her to, what Eddie had brought her to, what—

'It isn't simple, Izzy. I'm not saying that.' Finn was shaking his head. 'Relationships are complicated because people are complicated. Linear doesn't come into it day to day, but zoom out, and that's how the big picture looks.' Little shrug. 'You start off with someone, and go on until it falls apart.'

Rather bleak. But then again...

'I suppose, but it sounds quite sad, a bit cynical.'

He scoffed, turning his gaze to the sea. 'I don't make the rules.'

Bitterness in his voice, because of Janine, no doubt. Bitterness he must know she could hear...

She felt a tingle. Was he sending out a signal? Was this Finn now, trying to open a door?

If so, then she was right here, although best not to pounce. Rather, go slow. Rather, casually dip into her tote for the two bottles of water she had brought, and oh-so-casually hand him one…

'Here you go.'

He smiled. 'Thanks.' And then he was cracking the cap, giving her the twinkling side-eye. 'Just what I need after swallowing half the ocean at your fair hands.'

'If you're trying to send me on a guilt trip, heads up, it isn't working!'

And getting sidetracked into teasing was only going to pull her off course.

She uncapped her own bottle, using the moment to breathe. Then she shifted, angling herself toward him, trying to sound as if the thought had only just arrived in her head. 'You know, when you said just now that you don't make the rules, you sounded rather bitter.'

His bottle hand stilled mid-air, then lowered slowly as his gaze came to hers.

A pained gaze. Resistance in it. But she couldn't let it deter her. If he was hanging on to hurt so that it was still colouring his tone a year after his break-up, she couldn't sit here silent, couldn't not be moved, couldn't not want to listen, empathise, soothe him.

She dug in, levelling her gaze into his. 'Look, I know you said back there on the path that I've got enough on my plate already, but that edge to your voice was obviously because of Janine, and I can't just pretend I didn't hear it. Do you want to talk, get it off your chest? You've listened to me so much. Please, let me do the same for you now. Aren't we friends?'

His gaze broke apart, softening. 'Yes. We *are* friends, and I appreciate you noticing, reaching out, but I just…' Shaking his head. 'I just can't go there.'

So frustrating!

'Why, Finn? Is it a male thing? Is it that you don't want to come undone in front of me?'

His gaze flickered, signalling what, that she was on the right beat?

She licked her lips quickly, pressing her gaze into his, loading it with all the reassurance she could muster. 'I mean, if that's it, I get it. But it's all right. Whatever you want to throw at me is fine.' *Maybe a touch of humour…* 'I mean, look at me back there on the path just now, spitting fire! I already blazed the trail.'

His lips parted, and then he was looking at her, holding her gaze, shadows moving behind his eyes. A momentary glimmer. A spark. But then the spark fizzled and died.

He frowned. 'I'm sorry, Izzy. I just…'

A knot lodged in her chest. It was the wings of the stage all over again, wasn't it? Same flickering shadows in his eyes. Same retreat happening in his gaze. Same tingling behind her sinuses, same hot ache starting behind her lids, same feeling rising inside her—that she wasn't what he needed, wasn't good enough, was lacking something. And maybe it was reducing herself to ask him, but she didn't care anymore. She just wanted to know, needed to know...

'Is it me, Finn? Something about me?'

His gaze flared. 'For heaven's sake, Izzy, no!' Staring at her, on and on, until suddenly he turned, snatching his shirt off the top of his pack, shaking it out. 'I just don't *want* to talk about it, okay?'

Candid. Definitive. Final.

Nothing more to say.

Not to *her*, anyway...

She swallowed hard, pushing it all down, forcing her voice onto a level track. 'Okay. I'm sorry for asking. I won't ask again.'

His body tensed momentarily. Then he continued putting on his shirt. 'Look, Izzy, I don't want this to be—'

A ringtone sounded, cutting him off.

His eyes glanced into hers. 'It's mine. Sorry...' He snatched up his phone, getting to his feet. 'Hey, Jax. What's up?'

She took a sip from her bottle and capped it off. He was being summoned. That was what was up. Easy to piece together from his responses. Perhaps it was for the best.

And then he was ending the call, looking over, his expression strained. 'I'm sorry. I have to go lay down some drum tracks for this song we've been working on, "Beholden to You".' He bent to pick up his jeans. 'Jax says there're a couple of other songs shaping up too, which is good news, I guess.'

Trying to make conversation now, as if there wasn't this gaping hole between them. But perhaps that was for the best too. Pretending. Keeping things light and breezy and superficial. Safely distant. In fact, from now on, *safely distant* was going to be her modus, the way she was going to be.

Easier all round. Far less confusing.

She drew up a smile and aimed it at him. 'I'm sure it is, if things have been going slowly, I mean. Great if you can make some progress now.'

He nodded, then frowned. 'I realise it's not the best timing, but—'

'It's fine.' She forced up another smile. 'It's your job, after all, what you're actually here for.'

His gaze emptied a little. He turned away, pulling on his jeans and his boots, gathering up his towel, sorting himself out, his eyes fixed on what he was doing. 'Are you coming up?'

Seriously?

As if on any planet whatsoever she could have set off merrily back up the track with him now, chatting on about the weather and the state of the nation! Maybe that wasn't very mature of her, but there it was. Even *safely distant* had its limits.

She scooped a handful of beach grit, letting it run through her fingers. 'No. I think I'll hang on here for a while, go for another swim. Thanks for coming down, though...' Because if she didn't say it, she would only feel guilty later, and she had more than enough to contend with already without adding that to the mix.

'You don't have to thank me, Izzy. I *wanted* to come, remember?' Pocketing his phone. Shouldering his pack. Then his eyes found hers, his gaze soft and bruised. 'I'll text you later to check in, okay? Make sure the sharks didn't get you!'

Tears welled in her chest.

Damn him for making her want to cry and smile, for making her want him to stay as well as to be gone, safely distant!

She mustered up a smile from God knew where, together with an upbeat tone. 'Thanks. But you should scoot now. You've got drums to play, people waiting...'

'Yes, I have.' An unfathomable ripple crossed his gaze, and then he was turning, striding away, throwing up a hand. 'Catch you later, Iz.'

* * *

Later...

But what would *later* feel like now that there was this great big jagged tear in their cloth? How would it feel now, having to force distance between them all the time, having to keep Finn at arm's length?

Fresh tears seared her lids.

Miserable. Unnatural. Painful.

And it was all so stupid, this feeling that something was broken between them, because what was there to break? What was Finn to her anyway? A knight in shining armour, yes. A friend in need, definitely. A slick of balm for her soul, absolutely. But nothing more. For pity's sake, he had only dropped into her life again two days ago! For sure, back in the day, she had been a slave to the idea of him, but she was older now, wiser, and also still reeling from what happened with Eddie, still sorting through that wreckage. It shouldn't even have been possible for Finn to be cutting this deep with her, wielding this degree of torment after no time at all. But there it was.

She pressed her fingers to her eyes hard, then pulled in a breath, swapping her damp towel for her cover-up, settling her gaze on the sea.

Maybe it was down to the state she was in. Life had dealt her a kick, and Finn had stepped in, being kind, and so she had latched on to him, latched on too quickly and too tightly because he made everything better. The sky bluer. The sun warmer. Herself lighter, funnier, more present. She had got herself stupidly attached, wanting to be something to him in return so she could feel something coming back from him, so she could feel valued...

She rubbed her forehead. But seriously, what the hell for? Because there was no end game here. She and Finn were not an item, were not on the way to being one. It wasn't important to know all his ins and outs, his whole history. Clearly *that* was what he thought, was what he had been trying to convey with his flat-out refusal. Occam's razor! The most obvious explanation. And if she was sitting here feeling bruised now, then even if it wasn't exactly her fault, it was nevertheless—

'Iz?'

Her heart lurched.

Finn!

Back somehow, his eyes full, burning into hers, his shoulders heaving. 'I'm sorry. I didn't mean to hurt you, but I know I have, and I can't leave until I've made it right...'

CHAPTER THIRTEEN

Searching his face, and then suddenly tears rose in her eyes, driving a needle into his heart. 'But what about Jax? What about your recording?'

As if laying down a drum track could ever be more important than fixing this, than chasing those tears away.

'The recording can wait.'

'But Jax—'

'Can also wait. I texted him. He knows I'm delayed.'

Unavoidably, since his feet had refused to carry him more than ten yards up that path, refused because Izzy had taken his ham-fisted silence over Janine the wrong way, turned it inwards, into some imagined failing in herself, and he couldn't bear it.

Every step, words raining down on his head, twisting his insides into knots.

'Is it me, Finn? Something about me…?'

He had tried to tell her it wasn't, hadn't he? Not in the way that she thought, anyway. He had tried to be emphatic, lay the issue firmly at his own door, had come *this* close to caving when she had apologised in that stoic, wounded voice, promising not to ask him again. Then Jax had called. And in those few seconds, she'd changed, put on a brittle, smiling mask, found a few choice barbs to throw at him, like how playing the drums was his job, that it was what he was *really here* for. And he had thought, *fine!* In the sting of the moment, it had felt that maybe a little disruption to their flow would be no bad thing, would inject a healthy dose of distance between them.

His chest heaved. But God help him, he didn't *want* to be distant from Izzy, didn't want things to be sticky between them. And so here he was, to make amends, to do whatever it took to make things right, smooth things out.

At least she wasn't giving him the stiff mask treatment anymore…

He took a breath. 'Can I sit down?'

She nodded, lowering her gaze to her lap.

He dropped his pack, then sat down beside her. 'I'm sorry, Izzy. I didn't mean to upset you, never meant to hurt you.'

She took a little breath. Then her lips tightened. 'I know that.'

Heartening!

'Me holding back isn't a reflection on you, so please don't go thinking that.'

Her eyes jumped to his, glistening again. 'How am I not supposed to think that, though? Applying your Occam's razor thingy, it's the most obvious conclusion. I've trusted you with my stuff, opened up to you, but you won't do the same with me, so obviously you don't see me as someone you can talk to. Trust!'

His pulse exploded. So far off the mark it wasn't true! And if he was feeling *this* inflamed at the falseness of the accusation, could actually feel his blood bubbling, then what the hell was he holding out on her for anyway? Because, applying Occam's razor to this situation, if he was feeling *this* stirred, then he was already in over his head, wasn't he? So why not give up the fight and just damn well talk to her, give her the trust she was asking for? If the result was kindred spirits and greater closeness, then would that really be so bad? And if the worst happened, if he found himself sliding towards making some wrong move, then at least he could leave quickly, without impunity, because right now he was supposed to be in the recording studio and Izzy knew that.

He drew in a calming breath. It was all good. He could do this, turn this thing around…

'It's not the case, Iz, I swear.' He shifted, angling himself toward her so he could level his gaze into hers, so she would see he was for real. 'If you need proof, I'll deliver this time, I promise. Ask me anything you like.'

Her gaze filled his. 'You mean it? Anything?'

'Yes.'

A hundred times yes...

'Okay...' She shifted, turning herself fully to face him. 'What did Janine do that hurt you so badly?'

His chest sprouted a knot.

Going straight for the jugular!

But he had invited this in, had to keep his word to her now and open up.

'She stopped believing in us. In me. In the band.'

Izzy's forehead wrinkled. 'What's the band got to do with it?'

Seriously?

'Only everything! You've heard the expression "Love me, love my dog"?'

'You're saying the band's your dog.'

'As good as. I've never made any bones about that to anyone, to the women I've gone out with. When Jax and I started the band, we agreed to give it our best shot, put everything we'd got into making it. And now we have. But it's taken a lot of legwork. Years of playing gigs up and down the country. Pubs. Clubs. Grotty village halls.

Minor music festivals. Anywhere that would have us. Our mantra was exposure, exposure, exposure, because you have to be in it to win it.'

'So you were laser-focused?'

Nice way of putting it. 'Thanks for not saying *obsessive*.'

She gave a small smile, then tucked her hair behind her ears. 'But whatever we're calling it, you're saying that Janine had a problem with it?'

The knot in his chest flexed. 'Ultimately, yes. But the point is, she knew the score when we met. In fact, we met at a gig.'

'Okay...' Izzy's gaze tightened on his, prompting, but he didn't need prompting. The beginning was important, would help her understand the crushing pain of the end...

'It was circa two and a half years ago. We were playing a smallish venue up north. Jan was there to support one of her former service users. They were doing one of the late-night open mike sessions. She was a social worker, see, and worked with young people. We got talking. Swapped numbers. Just casually. But then, surprise, surprise, there she was at our next gig. Front row. Digging it. Cheering and clapping like we were the best band she'd ever heard.'

Brown eyes shining, gaze burning with admiration, full of faith, full of promise...

'We started seeing each other after that, even

though she lived up north, and I was down south. She'd come to wherever we were playing, spend the weekend, and it was great, the way she fitted in with us all, the way she could give Jax a run for his money in the verbal athletics department. I fell in love with her, thought she was in love with me too.'

Izzy blinked. 'But…?'

He felt his stomach shift. 'But a year down the line, she started complaining. Subtly, at first, wondering out loud why we were playing such and such a venue if we thought it was a dive, questioning the number of gigs we were playing and the way Jax was managing our schedule. I knew it was because she wanted us to spend more time together, away from the band, which was completely reasonable. So I tried. On the few weekends I had free, I'd go up to her place, or I'd take her away somewhere—walking in the lakes, or to the coast—but it wasn't enough. She wanted us to go away on a proper holiday like *normal* couples did, and I did want that too, but the band had commitments—'

'And you were committed to the band.' Izzy was nodding, empathy mounting in her gaze. 'I can see it must have been difficult. For both of you.'

'Yeah, but the difference is, I didn't criticise her for wanting what she wanted whereas she started criticising me for everything, notably for not pushing myself at work, for not taking my *proper* job seriously. Making *that* distinction, you know, as if she didn't damn well know that BioOnica was my cruise ship! And she didn't stop there. She started swiping at me for living in a rented flat, too.'

'Which I assume she didn't?'

'God no! Perish the thought!' He clawed up a handful of beach grit, squeezing it hard to feel its bite. '*She* owned a smart new-build place in Manchester, was a fully-fledged grown-up, whereas suddenly, instead of being a *dedicated, ambitious musician*—her actual words, by the way—I was a *fantasist* wasting my life on a dream that would *never happen*. I was a *man-child* who didn't want to grow up. I was *delusional*. The band were *always on the cusp* but never getting anywhere. Couldn't I see that? Could I not *read the room*? You name it, she laid it on me, bit by bit. And it hurt every time, because it was *my* dream, the one she'd started off supporting, the one I thought she believed in too.

'I'm not saying that being with me was easy, but I wasn't the one who changed. She was. And she'd say that was because we were stuck, weren't *moving on* with our lives. But *moving on* in Jan's book was marriage and kids. Me moving north, giving up the band and everything

I'd worked for, trading it all in for some safe job with *prospects*. And I didn't want to be a cog in any corporate machine, but I did want the rest, or at least I thought I did. So I held on, playing for time, I admit, because I could *feel* something in the air. The band was starting to cut some ice. Big Day were making overtures to us about playing support in Glasgow, but Jan said it was just more pie in the sky, that nothing would come of it, nothing would *actually* happen. I thought it was just another one of our typical arguments, that we'd kiss and make up like we always did. But that weekend, when I went to see her, she didn't kiss me. She gave me an ultimatum instead. It was either her or the band.'

Izzy's eyes welled. 'Oh, Finn…'

Beaming out empathy, freshening the hurt inside him, the shock, the devastation, bringing it all back to aching life. That moment. Jan's face, a stranger's face. Her gaze, a stranger's gaze.

He swallowed hard. 'I just stood there, you know. Stunned! I couldn't believe she'd do that to me, hold a gun to my head like that when she *knew* what the band meant to me, how hard we'd worked to get where we were. I couldn't believe that this was the person I'd shared my dreams with, fallen in love with.

'Anyway, that changed instantly, obviously. She'd killed my faith, killed us, killed everything.' The knot in his chest twisted tight. 'Even worse though, was that she got me questioning myself, doubting myself.'

Recognition surfaced in Izzy's gaze, along with a sudden fresh gleam of tears. 'Like me.' She swallowed. 'Been there, done that, got the T-shirt…'

His heart surged.

Kindred spirits.

'Exactly.' He let go of the grit in his hand, rubbing off the remnants on his jeans. 'I took a couple of very bad days over it, wondering if Jan was right after all, if I *was* actually a fantasist, if I'd spent the best part of a decade chasing a unicorn. I was so low, Iz. So down. I remember calling Carl, bending his ear.'

'What did he say?'

'God knows! I was drinking, somewhat out of it. To be honest, that whole week is still a bit of a blur. On the Saturday, I had Jan, wielding her ultimatum. Come Wednesday, Jax was getting a call from the *Sam Nelligan Show*. The band booked to play couldn't make it because their lead singer was sick. Nelligan had heard some of our stuff, apparently, and liked it. Could we make it to the studio for six o'clock the next day to play in front of a television audience?' He permitted himself a satisfying ripple of bitter triumph. 'So much for being delusional. So much for pie in the sky!'

'Too right.' Izzy gave a small smile. 'Nice to be vindicated, to have all your doubts quashed in a single stroke like that.' And then a frown filtered into her gaze. 'Did Janine get back in touch at all?'

His stomach soured. 'No. Not even to say congratulations. A nice touch, I thought. Didn't at all make me wonder how on earth I could have fallen for her in the first place, not that I'm bitter or anything...'

Izzy's head tilted. '*Are* you still bitter, genuinely?' Searching his face, his gaze. 'Because if you're still bitter a year after the end of an eighteen-month relationship, then—'

'What's it going to be like for you?' He felt his heart turning over for her. 'I hear you.'

But what to say? Lying wouldn't help her, or himself, not now that talking, emptying out the dregs of himself was feeling like a release, like a blessed relief. Besides, this was what she wanted, wasn't it? The full, unabridged version of what he'd been through, and he had promised to deliver it, the whole miserable kit and caboodle.

'Mostly, I'm fine...' He dipped his chin at her to make the point. '*Genuinely.* I'm over Janine, past caring. But if I let myself think about certain things, I can still feel bitter. Like if I think about us getting that call to go on Sam's show... Obviously it yanked me out of the doldrums pretty fast. We were all ecstatic! It was literally a dream come true. But not having someone of my own to share it with took some of the shine off, and I can still feel pretty sore at Janine about that.

'And afterwards, when everything started happening for us, it was rough being the only one without a significant other.' He felt a dip in his chest. 'I remember doing this radio show, and the DJ was asking us if our "other halves" were as excited as we were about the success of our first release. I had to own up to being single, and the numpty spun it into this whole thing about how I was available, which was just excruciating. If I let myself think about stuff like that, it can churn me up.'

'I'm not surprised.' Izzy sighed, and then she sighed again. 'At least I'll get to spend my bitter years in private...'

His heart squeezed.

Too bleak!

Not a thought he could let her dwell on...

'Or maybe you'll get past it all sooner than you think. I mean, break-ups aren't one-size-fits-all. You've got a long history with Eddie, shared a home. Separating means you're going to have to talk to each other.'

Her brows arched. 'And this is somehow meant to be a ray of light?'

'Yes! Even if you're only talking about who gets the air fryer, it's communication after the fact, which might help you come to terms with things. I mean, if Jan had ever reached out to me afterwards, not to resurrect us but just to say, "Good on you," just to acknowledge that I'd been right to keep pushing for the dream, I think I'd have found closure much sooner than I did.'

Izzy nodded, and her gaze opened out, all warm. 'Well, for what it's worth, *I* really admire you, Finn. Working so hard, keeping at it.' She gave him a little smile. 'I've never wanted anything that badly, never felt *that* passionate about…' And then, as if she had decided that the words weren't worth saying, she exhaled, turning her gaze to the sea. 'We're a sad pair, aren't we?'

He felt his lips trying to twitch. 'Well, we are *now*.' He gave her big toe a tweak to shake her loose. 'See! This is what comes of sharing my woes. I *did* warn you.'

Her gaze swung back. 'Oh, so this is *my* fault?'

His heart stilled. And there it was again, that lovely teasing light in her eyes.

He felt a smile loosening in his cheeks, lightness skipping through him. They were back on track. Better than before. The air between them softer. Warmer.

He looked at her. 'Yes. Totally your fault…'

Her lips curved. 'Well, maybe so, but it means a lot that you told me, Finn, that you came back.' She was blinking now, welling up, making his own eyes burn. His chest. His throat. And then she took a little nodding breath. 'I'm so glad you did.'

He swallowed hard. 'So am I.'

No need to say more—as if he even could—that the way they had left things before had felt intolerable, wrong in all the ways wrong could be. It was already communicated. Understood. Everything shuttling between them. Everything, and then something more, something that…

He shook himself. Something that he needed to leave well alone. And on the subject of leaving…

He drew up a smile. 'And now that I've spilled all my beans—'

'You need to go.' Nodding, sweet understanding in her eyes. 'You've got people to see, drums to play, all that *being famous* stuff to do.'

He felt a fresh smile breaking. 'I don't know what all the *being famous* stuff is, but you're right, I need to go beat the hell out of some drums.' He got to his feet. 'Are you going to come up too?'

She shook her head. 'Not yet.' But she was getting up all the same, pushing her hair back with her hand. 'I'm going to go for another swim first.'

'Braving the sharks?'

Her brows quirked. 'Just so you know, that isn't wearing remotely thin.'

Like the lovely light in her eyes wasn't wearing thin, or the sweet, heartbreaking sight of her. And suddenly, simply saying goodbye didn't feel like enough, and maybe she was feeling it too, because in the next moment they were somehow moving, flowing together into a hug. And she felt so right in his arms, her body softening against him, arms going around him all warm and tight. He closed his eyes, giving in to sensation. Such connection! Affection! Feeding his soul, it felt like, his spirit, stirring golden feelings around inside him, so many that he couldn't pin a single one down, except for the desperate one that never wanted this to end. She wasn't signalling that she wanted it to end either. Rather she was snuggling in as if she belonged there.

Oh God! But if he didn't end it, pull away right now, the urge to bury his lips into her salt-sticky hair would be too overwhelming, and he couldn't let himself be overwhelmed, couldn't let himself be *that* weak, because it would spoil everything.

'Right then.' He bore down, forcing himself to straighten, felt her disengaging, and then they were blessedly apart again, Izzy smiling up at him, her eyes twinkling into his.

'You're a very good hugger, Finn Falco.'

God help him, that smile on her, making him want to go for a replay, but replaying the hug was *not* an option. Only smiling back, forcing up a casual tone…

'You're not such a bad hugger yourself, Izzy Valentine.'

And now, it was a case of picking up his pack, forcing his feet to walk before the temptation to linger could get the better of him. 'Catch you later.'

Her voice came chasing after him. 'As long as the sharks don't catch me first.'

He felt a smile catching at his lips. Teasing him to the end, but he couldn't turn and look at her, because if he did…

He threw up a hand instead. 'Wearing thin now, Iz. Wearing *mighty* thin!'

CHAPTER FOURTEEN

BUT *HE* WASN'T wearing thin.

More the opposite…

And watching him walk away was probably a bad move, because doubtless he could feel her eyes on his back, feel the fond weight of her gaze. Then again, why worry? It wasn't as if she hadn't already given herself away in spades, welling up in front of him like that the second he arrived, wearing all of her emotions on her face. How much it meant that he had come back—*for her*—to make things right. And if all that had somehow passed him by, then he would have definitely felt it coming through her when they hugged…

She pressed her lips together. Disappearing now into the trees. Going. Going.

Gone.

She drew in a breath and turned, dropping back down onto her mat.

That hug…

Heavenly!

Moving together at exactly the same time, his arms wrapping round her so tight, drawing her right into his chest. Warmth coming through him. Affection. Relief as well, maybe. All the things she was feeling too, wanted him to feel flowing through her, flowing out through her arms, through her body…

Could a hug be a whole conversation? Because that was what it had felt like. Like a conversation they were having. Like a promise they were making, a fence they were mending. *Friends again!* Closer. Fonder. Better. And underneath, running deep like water, there had been that feeling of peace, of home, of belonging, that tantalising sense that he was feeling it too.

She dug her fingers into the beach. Unless she was getting carried away, reading too much into that silent conversation. Reading peace and home and belonging into Finn because Eddie had robbed her of those things, and Finn was here, filling the void Eddie had left, constantly filling it with warmth and kindness. Filling it with his trust and his attentiveness. Putting the band on hold—*for her*—so he could come back and open up to her. Later, he had been like, *Love me, love my dog*. Later, he had been all about how the band always came first…

Her heart surged. But today, he had put her

first, hadn't he? Put her first, then held her tight as if she mattered to him. Counted!

But counted for what? Mattered how much?

Maybe she shouldn't even have been asking herself that question, but how not to? How *not* to be curious when this was Finn, the one she had been crazy about at school, the only one she had ever wanted to be with. How could she make herself not ask the question, make herself *not* feel stirred up by the possibility that, after all these years, he could maybe like her now, like her in *that* way…

Pulling her in so close and tight like she was a precious thing, his body moulding to hers, whispering to hers, it felt like.

Oh God!

Was that why she was tingling all over, why she was—

Stop!

What was she doing?

Reality check!

She wasn't a prospect worth contemplating by anyone right now, least of all by Finn. Not after Janine! And not after giving him a front-row seat to the entire gamut of her chaos. Her drunken tabletop dancing. Her ridiculous fling fixation. Her ugly vengefulness. Her despondency, and her inappropriate flirting, and all her crippling devastation. She couldn't even eat a stupid ice cream without dripping it all over her stupid dress.

Reality check!

Izzy Valentine was *not* a catch. She was a mess, inside and out. So delusional and needy that here she was, actually imagining herself some desire into Finn's hug, talking herself into Finn liking her in *that* way, when what was *obviously* going on here was that he was simply looking out for her because he was kind, and because also, Carl had asked him to.

He had only hugged her because he had the vision and sensitivity to see that she needed it, needed some bolstering warmth. And because he was a good soul, he probably *had* felt mightily relieved that they were mended, back on track. That was what she must have picked up on while they were hugging, the whisper she had caught and misread—*obviously* misread—because he had pulled away first, hadn't he? Straightening. Releasing her. Drawing it all to a close when, if he had been remotely into her in the other way, he surely would have used the opportunity to…

She blew out a breath and brushed the grit off her hands. That was the writing on the wall, right there. But it was for the best. Genuinely! Because say if Finn had made a move, tried to kiss her, what would she have actually done? For a second it would have felt amazing, like a dream come true, for sure, but only for a second. And then it would have felt too big, like too much to deal with, because she had all this other stuff to contend with. A life with Eddie to dismantle. A life of her own to begin. All the unknowns to tie down—where she was at, what she wanted, who she was. The whole pitiful mess of herself to sort out. Her failings. Her flaws. All of her stupid weaknesses and blindnesses. She needed to fix those, fix herself—*find* herself—before she could even think about starting over. And to fix herself, she needed to stop all her pointless mooning and get on her own case, start looking after herself as per Carl's instructions. Rest and recuperation. Health and well-being. Those were things she could actually *do* something about while she was here.

Project Izzy Valentine!

She stripped off her cover-up and got to her feet. So first a swim to get Finn out of her head and the endorphins pumping. Then a trip into town for supplies. Healthy food to cook. Oh, and also, aqua shoes.

She braced and stepped off her mat, wincing as her foot sank.

Definitely, *definitely*, aqua shoes!

CHAPTER FIFTEEN

STILL NOT ANSWERING!

Finn threw his phone back down on the bed and gave his hair another vigorous scrub with the towel.

All very well joking about sharks, non-existent sharks by the way, but even so, he could feel his nerves starting to jangle.

Six hours straight in the studio, and the first thing he had done when he came out was text Izzy—just to check in. And no, he hadn't expected her to text back immediately or anything, but this was coming up to two hours later now, which he knew because he had been faffing on his laptop for an hour, ordering birthday presents for Ma and Maisie and his sister Niamh. Then he had called his brother Liam for a catch-up, and *then* he had gone for a shower to wash off the beach salt that was still clinging to him from this morning. In all that time, there had been no reply from Izzy. And phoning wasn't getting him anywhere, even though he had tried three times. As likely as not, her phone was buried in her bag, or on charge in another room. Likely as not, there was nothing at all to worry about— but see, that was the problem now with Izzy...

Worrying about her.

Thinking about her.

He went to hang his towel back up.

Pretty much all of the time, thinking about her, and about that hug. Replaying the way it had felt. *So good...* The vibes coming through. *So sweet...* Reliving the warm way she had melted into him, held him tight, giving no sign she would ever pull away. Leaving the pulling away part to him, leaving him as the one battling temptation, finding the strength inside himself to do that. Thinking about that short walk across the beach to the path, reliving the pressure of her gaze, the tug of it.

The tug of her...

Undeniable. Tugging at him right now. Putting a notion into his head to go round there to see that she was all right. And he could tell himself it was because Carl had asked him to keep an eye on her, that it was a duty call, but that would be stretching the truth too thin, to a breaking point, because the truth was that he wanted to go for himself. Because he cared about her. Liked her. Liked being with her. Because he *wanted* to see her, just to see that teasing light in her eyes, feel that tingling buzz shuttling back and forth between them. Kindred spirits. Fellow feeling. All the good stuff, all the magic…

And yes, maybe it went against *no woman, no cry*, but what could he do? His heart didn't want him to stay away from Izzy. He had been there, done that, got the T-shirt, stayed away from her when he was sixteen, seventeen, eighteen, hadn't he? Forced himself to walk right past her at their leavers' ball when all he had wanted to do was stop and take her in, take in her loveliness…that red velvet dress she'd had on, her hair swept up, showing the delicate lines of her neck, and her lips reddened with lipstick, so kissable, and her lovely face, everything about her so utterly, utterly beautiful. Maybe if he hadn't walked past her that night, had asked her to dance instead, she might never have got involved with Eddie, might have been his now, sharing this crazy life with him.

He hunted out clothes, put them on. Or maybe she would have turned him down and nothing at all would have come of it. But what was certain was that she had held him like she meant it on the beach this morning, and he had felt the vibes he had felt. And, no, it didn't mean he had read those vibes right, or that she was into him in *that* way, didn't mean she was ready for him in any way whatsoever, because of course she wasn't. *Couldn't be.* Not now.

But the way she had held him had got him

thinking, thinking that *now* wasn't forever. This hurting time would pass. Inevitably she would heal. And maybe if they were close when that moment came, close friends, something *could* happen between them…

He could wait for her—*would!*—could bide his time, play the long game.

Might be better in any case, give him time to get used to this freaky fame thing, buy a house somewhere, get ready for starting over.

He went to the mirror, setting to with the brush, tying his hair back up. At least he knew now that Carl wouldn't be an issue. He felt a smile coming. Carl thought he was a catch, after all. Horse's mouth! Maybe Carl hadn't been thinking of him as a catch for Izzy when he had said it, but what was to say that, if Finn put in the time with her, proved himself a steady and reliable friend to her first, Carl wouldn't come to see him as a contender, the right kind of guy? The kind who would worry if he hadn't heard from her in almost eight hours. The kind who would think nothing of putting beers with the lads on hold so he could go see that she was all right.

He pulled in a breath. A guy like the one he was looking at in the mirror.

A guy like Finn Falco!

CHAPTER SIXTEEN

'I SEE YOU'RE upping the ante…'

Her heart double-skipped.

Finn. Eyeing the knife in her hand, his hair fetchingly awry from pulling off his helmet.

Teasing her of course, harking back to the pepper mill, but why was he here? Not that she minded. It was good to see him. She felt a smile coming. Always good to see him. A lovely surprise…

'I was cooking—chopping stuff—and didn't think to leave the knife behind.'

Twinkling eyes came to hers. 'So, I'm not in mortal danger?'

In those black jeans and that dark long-sleeved tee, he might well have been, once upon a time, or rather, *she* might well have been. That was, if she hadn't spent the afternoon thinking hard about herself, about how she had never really been alone, never learned how to be a strong and independent woman, existing for herself, on her own terms. She had fallen in so quickly with Eddie, gone with *his* flow instead of finding her own, finding herself. This was her new declared mission now. Self-discovery. Self-care. Living for herself. By herself. And so...

'No. You're perfectly safe.'

He cocked an assessing eyebrow. 'As you clearly are, too.'

Her heart paused. Which meant what, exactly? Unless...

Oh no!

She felt a sudden crushing sensation in her chest. 'You came to check on me?'

He gave a little shrug. 'You weren't picking up.'

Because she had only gone and done it again, hadn't she? Left her stupid phone in her bag, and her bag on the bedroom chair, out of sight, out of earshot. The very thing Carl had told her *not* to do. And now Finn was here, had probably felt obliged to come because Carl had asked him to keep tabs on her. And what kind of welcome was this? Knife, brandished! Half-cracked door!

She pulled the door wide open. 'I'm so sorry. My phone is in my bag. I didn't hear it. I feel terrible.'

'Don't...' He shook his head. 'It's fine.'

So why didn't it feel fine? Why did it feel as though more was...

She licked her lips quickly. 'Would you like to come in?'

The least she could do. She felt a tingle. Or was it? She was making dinner, after all, could easily make extra. And maybe it went slightly against her new strong, independent woman mindset to be offering to feed a man, but for heaven's sake, Finn was a friend, had come round to make sure she was still alive. How could she not offer?

She looked at him. 'What I mean is, have you eaten? Full disclosure—I'm not a patch on Carl in the kitchen, but you're welcome to stay for dinner if you'd like. If you're hungry...'

His lips parted. 'I wasn't... I wouldn't want to...' Then his focus shifted, his features drawing into a sudden frown. 'I think something's burning.'

Her heart seized.

Oh God!

The courgettes!

She ran to the kitchen, pulled the pan off the hob, but it was too late.

Then Finn was beside her, looking into the pan as well, a smile twitching at the corners of his mouth. 'What were they originally?'

She felt her belly kink. How could he be making her laugh when she was staring into the abyss, feeling the prickling humiliation of yet another epic fail? But somehow, he was.

'Courgettes. Gently sautéed with pine nuts and garlic, wouldn't you know?'

'Ah!' He set his helmet down. 'I'm really sorry, Izzy.'

What?

'Why are *you* sorry?'

'I distracted you.'

'No! You very *kindly* came to check on me.'

'Okay, but you've now got cremated courgettes.' His hands went to his head, retying his hair, and then he pushed his sleeves up. 'Can I prep some more for you, or make something else?'

Wow!

She looked at him. 'You cook?'

He rolled his eyes. 'Yes, I cook.' He broke into his warm, easy smile. 'That summer I spent in Tuscany, I didn't *only* ride my uncle's scooter. I put in some serious hours in the kitchen too.'

God help her! Not only drop dead gorgeous, kind, funny, sweet, and a talented drummer but *also* a dab hand in the kitchen. Maybe it wasn't very strong and independent of her, but she kind of wanted to see him in action.

'Do you have a speciality?'

'One or two…' And then his gaze fell to the

chopping board. 'Did you have a plan for these aubergines?'

'Not as yet, but I'm guessing you do.'

'Maybe.' He looked up, his eyes merry. 'Can I check out what else you've got in your fridge?'

As if she could refuse him anything when he was looking at her like this, when she could feel those little sparks shuttling between them again…

'You may, although I have a couple of conditions.'

'Which are?'

'One, that you stay for dinner, because no way am I letting you cook if you're not also going to eat.'

He smiled. 'Okay, done! What's your other condition?'

'That you let me help you.'

His smile faded a little. 'O—kay, but you're not to do any sautéing.'

Seriously?

'But the courgettes were *your* fault, Finn! You distracted me, remember?'

Laughing. 'No, I *very kindly* came by to check on you, *remember*?'

Teasing. Laughing into her eyes. Making the moment stretch, the sparks fly faster. Sparks she shouldn't even have been feeling, letting herself feel, that she needed to stop feeling right now, because she was a strong and independent woman, and Finn was a friend. *Only* a friend.

She faked a withering look and fired it at him. 'Oh, go lose yourself in the contents of the fridge. And while you're there, grab yourself a beer, or there's white wine if you want. If you prefer red, I can do that, too.'

'Red sounds good. If it needs opening, I'll get to it in a sec...'

And then he was turning, rooting around in the fridge, humming to himself, which was adorable. As for his neat rear in those black jeans...

She tore her eyes away, getting glasses down, the wine, the corkscrew, channelling strength and independence for all she was worth. 'So how did your recording session go?'

'Really well, thanks.' He closed the fridge and came back to the worktop, setting down onions, more garlic, parmesan, tomatoes. 'We finally nailed this track we've been working on, got it mixed, so all in all, good progress.' His gaze lighted on the wine. 'This one?'

'Yep.' She handed him the corkscrew. 'How far along are you with the new album?'

The cork gave a restrained pop. 'Not as far as we should be.'

Which he had alluded to that first night as well, hadn't he? And she hadn't asked him about it then because she had been bent on escaping, but now…

She slid the glasses toward him. 'How come?'

He poured, his eyes glancing into hers. 'How long have you got?'

That face… This moment… The evening stretching ahead of them…

Just two friends hanging out. Nothing more than that. It didn't mean she wasn't strong. Didn't mean she wasn't independent. Didn't mean she couldn't let go and enjoy Finn's company, let go and smile.

'I've got as long as it takes.'

CHAPTER SEVENTEEN

Izzy bent to set her glass down on the stones. 'Talking of music, I forgot to put some on.'

As if it mattered. Because what could be better than the sound of the cicadas trilling, and the low shush of wavelets breaking on the beach below them? In fact, what could be better than this, period? Lazing on loungers in the glow of the solar lights, talking and teasing, finishing off the last of the wine, wine he shouldn't really have been drinking. But so what, if it meant walking back to Horvat's place? It wasn't far. And it wouldn't be the first time in his life that he'd had to hoof it home after a night out. Better *that* than not partaking, spoiling the convivial flow…

'It's cool, Iz.' He smiled at her. 'I'm okay with just this…'

'No!' She shook her head. 'It's nice to have music.' She swung off her lounger and giggled. 'I can't believe I'm saying that to *you*, of all people!' And then she was off, heading back inside, hair tumbling past the narrow straps of her vest, skirt dancing around her ankles.

Izzy...

So lovely.

Delightful!

He leant back and closed his eyes. Such a great evening. Unexpected! But he wasn't complaining. Her burnt offerings had given him the perfect opportunity to step into the breach, start clocking up the long game brownie points…

He felt a smile spreading into his cheeks. What a show he had put on! He had been like one of those puffed-up male jungle birds in a nature programme, displaying to the female to woo her, except *his* display had consisted of rapid onion dicing, tomato skinning and garlic smashing. All the knife skills. Everything he had learned in his uncle's hotel kitchen. And it had done the trick. Izzy had seemed impressed, made all the right appreciative noises from her delegated station, grating the parmesan, in between teasing him, of course.

And she listened to his lowdown on the band. How Taylor and Dobs were mates but were given to locking horns. How Jax was always chasing perfection, which sometimes got in the way of a good tune. How Matt didn't have the skill set to deal with that, or the patience for Dobs and Taylor's antics. How the four of them could end up going at each other, and how Finn didn't enjoy any of it.

'Too similar to your noisy siblings, by any chance?' Izzy had said, looking at him with that recognition in her eyes. *Understanding.* Showing that she had been paying attention that day he'd mentioned it…

He caught his breath. And paying attention this morning too, clearly, because *this* was only the intro to 'Damned If I Do' by Big Day striking up through the outdoor speakers.

He felt his hands moving, beating imaginary drums, his feet going for imaginary pedals.

'I thought you'd appreciate this one.' Izzy was coming back across the terrace, chuckling at him, smiling.

His heart gave. Where to even begin with the appreciation? For *her*, for the music, for this whole lovely evening. But he couldn't go overboard showing it.

Long game buddy, remember?

He scooped up his glass from the stones, returning her smile. 'A great track. Good choice!'

'What are Big Day like, then?' She sat back down. 'As people, I mean?'

'They're great! Decent guys. Nice to be around.'

Her eyes filled with an admiring glow. 'Such a world you live in now, Finn.' She picked up her glass, took a sip, then broke into another wide smile. 'But oh my God, what's blowing my mind more right now is that totally *divine* thing you made for dinner! What's it called again?'

So much gratitude for so little...

'That very *simple* dish I made is called melanzane alla parmigiana.'

Her gaze sparkled. 'Oh, I love the way you sound when you say it. Your accent is like *proper* Italian.'

If only she knew...

He shook his head. 'Meanwhile, the whole Italian side of my family laughs at my accent. They figure I'm a cockney.'

'No!' Her eyes widened, disbelieving. Horrified look. And then her lips curved up again. 'If they think *you're* cockney, I wonder what they'd make of *my* accent.' She ran a tongue over her lower lip. 'Mel-a-something a la parmee-jah-nah.'

Too funny!

'Listen carefully. It's melan-zane alla par-migiana.'

Her eyes locked on his, deadly, comically serious. 'Mel-ahn-zah-nay alla par-mee-jarn-ah.'

He felt a smile coming and sipped his wine to hide it. 'You're getting there with the accent. Just emphasize the zed sound more...'

'Okay.' She took a hefty sip from her own

glass, then drew in a breath. 'Melan-*zah*-nah alla par-mee-jarn-ah...' She frowned at her glass. 'I don't think the wine is helping.'

As if it mattered anyway!

'*Va tutto bene...*' He let his smile loosen. 'It's all good. Your pronunciation is improving.'

She scoffed. 'Well that's not saying much. I set a very low bar.'

His heart pinched.

Way to kill the joy!

He set his glass down. 'Don't do that, Izzy.'

'Don't do what?' She shook her head, shrugging as if she was genuinely bewildered.

He swung his legs off the lounger so he could sit up and face her. 'Don't put yourself down like that. You do it far too much.'

Staring at him, and then her lips tightened. 'No, I don't.'

'You *do*. All the time.' He leant his arms on his thighs to put himself closer to her, so she would take in what he was saying. 'Maybe you don't realise you're doing it—'

'Because I'm *not* doing it, that's why!'

So stubborn!

'You *are*, Izzy!' And if it meant spelling it out to her, then so be it because she needed to hear it, be aware, so she could jolly well *stop* doing it, *stop* raining on her own parade. 'It's like this morning, when we were swimming... I said we should race each other, and you started up this whole thing about how there wasn't any point, that you weren't a strong swimmer like Carl, that you didn't get your distance badges like he did. Meanwhile, the truth is, you swim like a fish!'

Looking at him, biting her lips.

At least she was listening…

'And when you were talking about your job, practically the first thing you said after the part about how you hadn't progressed was that you didn't know if you had it *in you* to be more than you are at the moment.' He felt a tingle, yet another example coming to mind. 'And just this evening, inviting me to dinner, literally in the same breath, you were warning me that you weren't a patch on Carl in the kitchen, which considering the only thing he's ever made for me is a cheese and chilli jam toastie, seems highly unlikely…' Her lips parted, gearing up to speak, but he could see what was coming, and he wasn't having it. 'Forget the courgettes. I distracted you, so they burned. That's cause and effect, not lack of skill—'

'I know that, Finn!' Cutting in, blinking. 'I'm not a total loser—'

His blood rose. 'But see! There you go again, assuming *that's* what I'm thinking, using *that* language. It's like *you've* decided you're a loser, put yourself in that box. Even at school—'

Gah!

So *not* where he had meant to go. But he had, somehow, and now Izzy was looking at him keenly, her gaze searching, her mouth working.

'What do you mean by that? You didn't even know me at school.'

Not for lack of wanting to! But this wasn't the time for that particular revelation. Rather, he needed to bite the bullet that he had just shot into his own foot, and hit her with some hopefully happy home truths…

'I know I didn't. But remember that show we did?'

Apprehension flickered through her gaze, then she shrugged. 'Vaguely. What about it?'

'Well, I assume you wanted to be in it, since you were always there at the rehearsals, but it always seemed to me like you were trying to hide behind Jess and Millie, as though you didn't think you were—'

Izzy cut in. 'I don't know where you're going with this, Finn, but so you know, I actually *didn't* want to be there.' And then she was pushing her free hand through her hair, setting her glass down, rearranging herself into a cross-legged position. 'Jess and Millie were the ones who wanted to do it, wouldn't give over nagging at me until I agreed to do it with them. They picked that awful song, said we had to do the stupid dance to go with it—'

He put up his hand. 'That's not… The *point* I'm trying to make is that for all your hiding and not wanting to be there, for all that you clearly didn't think you were any good, you were, in fact, a million times better than the other two.'

Her lips came together, her eyes searching each of his in turn, as if she was looking for a punchline. Then her gaze cleared, softening somewhat. 'You genuinely thought that?'

His heart turned over. God help him, how much did he want to take her face into his hands right now? But he couldn't.

Long game, remember?

He nodded instead, smiling into her eyes. 'Absolutely! Better voice. Better rhythm. You had more grace in your little fingernail than the other two put together.' He pressed his gaze into hers so she'd see the truth in it. 'You were the best, Iz, but I'll bet it never crossed your mind that you were, did it?'

Her lids fluttered. 'No…' And then she was looking down, playing with her fingers, her voice thickening a little. 'I thought I was terrible. I felt like a complete idiot.'

And there went his heart, turning over again. 'Well, you didn't look like one. You shone. And you need to start believing that about yourself, that you *deserve* your place on the stage, that you can shine as brightly as the next person.'

Her eyes snapped up. 'Not so easy believing *that* when you've spent your whole life being outshone at every turn, trying to curb expectation so that no one will compare you to your—' And then her whole body stiffened, her eyes widening, her gaze turning inwards as if she was caught up in a realisation, the very one he himself had referenced how many times earlier without ever properly locking it down, without ever quite pulling it together…

Carl!

His heart pulsed. This was all about Carl.

And now Izzy was setting her feet back down on the terrace, reaching for her glass again, shaking her head a little as if she was trying to make sense of it herself.

'I remember always wanting to be like Carl.' Her eyes came to his. 'When I was little, I mean.' She took a sip from her glass and set it back down, a smile ghosting over her lips. 'He could light up a room just by being in it. It felt like his eyes beamed light out, his smile, his skin, even. He could switch it on, you know. Still can. And he was so quick and clever at everything.'

She passed her hands over her face. Then she was looking at him again, a wet gleam at the corners of her eyes. 'Everything came so easy to Carl.'

Which he knew, had witnessed for himself. Top at maths. Top at science. Good at sports. So many talents, so much shine. Hard to compete with that. He had never bothered trying, as he wasn't built that way, or maybe growing up with so many brothers and sisters had simply inured him to that kind of rivalry, especially with a friend. But for Izzy…

Frowning now. 'We'd go to the play park and, I don't know when it started, but it got so that if Carl made for the swings, I'd run to the roundabout, because he could always swing higher than me, and I didn't want anyone comparing us.' She shook her head. 'Not that I rationalised it that way then. I was just a kid, but I can see it now, the way I was, what it's led to…'

All of it coming into painful focus now. And Finn's gaze too, in focus, holding hers, drawing words up from some dark well inside her…

'I concentrated on arts because Carl was into science, always swam in the shallow end because Carl liked the deep end. I chose books over sports because Carl was into sports. I separated myself from him in every way I could because I didn't know how to hold my own against him.' Her heart rolled. 'And *that's* why we were never close, growing up, like everyone expected us to be, because *I* wouldn't let him in. It's all my fault. Just like what happened with Eddie was my fault too.'

'Dumping you at the altar?' Finn's mouth set hard. 'I don't see how that's *your* fault—'

Her body flashed hot. 'That was just the outcome! But the *fault* was all mine because I didn't love him.' Oh, how the scales were falling from her eyes now. 'I never loved him, Finn. Not in the right way. I can admit it now. I took up with Eddie because he liked me, *chose* me, and it felt good to be chosen, to be noticed. He was nice, and he was kind, and he made me feel like I counted, like I mattered. When I took him home that first time, I could see Mum and Dad waking up to me, looking at me differently because I'd snagged this great guy with amazing prospects, this guy whose family had an estate in the country and a rather superb maisonette flat in Chelsea. And I *liked* seeing that approval in their eyes, *liked* the way our families gelled, *liked* that Carl wasn't part of our little club, that I had something special of my own…'

Damn her eyes for welling up like this but she couldn't hold her tears in now, not with this weight pressing down on her chest, all this guilt…

'But it wasn't special, and Carl could see it.

And because he's a good person, a kind, caring, wonderful brother, in spite of the way I was with him growing up, he tried to warn me, tried to talk some sense into me. I threw it back in his face because I didn't want to hear it, probably because, on some subliminal level, I knew he was right, and I couldn't bear to concede that. And because I couldn't, I've caused Eddie pain, and Carl pain, and my family, and myself. Now here I am offloading to you yet again, when you've probably had it up to here with—'

Finn's hands seized her shoulders. 'Would you please stop telling me what I have and haven't had enough of!' And then his grip softened, his eyes filling with tender light. 'I'm here for you, Izzy, okay? I *want* to be here, *want* you to offload if it helps. And whatever you think of yourself, what I *know* is that you're so much better than you think you are.'

Her heart went still. Was this real? Could this really be Finn Falco looking at her like this, saying these words to her? Was this really *his* hand lifting to her cheek, *his* thumb wiping her tears away?

'You're a good singer, Izzy. A good dancer. A good swimmer. A good diver.' A smile touched his lips. 'Very good at fencing, even without the right equipment. You're smart. And you're funny, lovely to be with...' His fingers stilled as his gaze deepened. Then they were moving again, gently tracing the line of her cheekbone, stirring a sweet, pulsing ache inside her. 'You're lovely, Izzy, beautiful inside and out. Surely you know that?'

Her throat caught. *Beautiful…*in *his* eyes. Eyes that were dropping to her mouth now, openly, the way they had in the wings so long ago. And she had stayed still then, waiting for a word, for lightning to strike. Waiting, not seizing the moment, not reaching for what she wanted because she didn't rate herself, didn't believe he could like her in that way. But now every signal he was sending out seemed to suggest that…

'Finn?'

His eyes jerked up, and time slowed.

Desire in his gaze. Molten amber. Burning. Real!

One hundred percent, *definitely* real…

Her heart pulsed. Everything she had ever wanted. Right here. And maybe it was madness to be acting now, but she couldn't seem to stop herself. She could feel her hands lifting, taking hold of his face, feel herself moving toward him, reaching up, taking his lips with hers. Soft, warm, perfect lips…

She closed her eyes.

Oh God!

The taste of him!

'Izzy…' He pulled away a fraction, but only a fraction, his eyes searching hers. 'What are you doing?'

As if it wasn't obvious!

'I'm kissing you.'

A ripple moved through his gaze, and then his hand moved, curling around her nape, drawing her in. 'Oh, Izzy…' Groaning into her mouth, even as his tongue was invading it, sliding against hers. Expert strokes. Drawing such flames through her. Heat like she had never felt it before. Torching her veins. Melting her bones, her blood, her core.

Closer!

As if she had said it out loud—*had she?*—he gripped her around the waist and lifted her onto his lap, pushing her thighs apart, drawing her in hard against him. Then his mouth was on hers again, kissing slow, then deep, then deeper still.

Such a feeling! *Sublime.* Like spiralling through space, weightless, everything turning on sensation. The tender warmth of his lips. The soft punishing grain of his tongue. The fresh scent of his skin. The softness of his beard. The hard, tantalising length of him.

She pushed herself against him, twisting her hands into his hair, taking control of the kiss. How to even begin to get enough of *this*? Of *him*!

Suddenly he was pulling back, pushing her

hair away from her neck, burying his lips there, his breath hot against her skin, his voice thick, messy. 'I want you, Izzy.'

Her blood surged. Not as much as she wanted him. All of him. Everything. The very breath from his lungs. Desire so strong she couldn't articulate it, desire reaching back a decade, coming to desperate, trembling life inside her…

Nipping at her neck with his teeth now, following with his tongue, his large hands moving over her body. Warm hands, hands she wanted to feel against her skin.

As if she had said that out loud too, he slipped a hand under her vest, working it upward to her breast.

She felt a groan escaping as his fingers found her nipple, teasing it through the lace of her bra.

'Do you like that, Iz?'

She closed her eyes, trying to talk through the sensations his clever fingers were wreaking on her body. 'That's a dumb question, Finn.'

'So that's a yes.'

She met his gaze. 'Yes, it's a yes.'

He gave a hazy smile, then leaned her backward, his fingers splaying between her shoulder blades to support her weight as he pulled up her vest and took her nipple into his mouth through the lace.

She felt her back arching involuntarily, her breath coming in short bursts.

Too heavenly!

Mouth. Fingers. Mouth again. She could feel her body trembling, aching, words escaping from her lips like they had never escaped with Eddie.

'Oh my God, Finn...'

He stopped, his head lifting. 'I guess that means you like this too?'

'Affirmative.'

'Excellent.' His fingers tugged the lace away, and then he was moving again, his mouth soft and wet around her hardness, his tongue a sweet, blinding torment. She felt a gasp working up her throat, breaking free as his hand moved again, sliding between her legs.

'Finn, please...'

His head jerked up. 'You want me to stop?'

'No!' *A thousand times no!* She pushed at his shoulders, forcing him to straighten so she could meet his gaze squarely, so she could kiss him again. 'I want you to take me to bed...'

CHAPTER EIGHTEEN

Different ceiling. Different bedding…

Finn caught his breath. Oh, but of course, this was Izzy's room, wasn't it? Izzy's bed!

Izzy…

He felt his heart rising and turned over, felt it promptly crashing back down.

Gone!

He touched the sheet where she had been.

Cold!

As if she had been gone for ages.

He rolled up, pulse drumming. 'Izzy?'

Silence.

No water running. No kitchen sounds. No music.

Weird!

Giving him the jitters.

He threw off the covers and got up, trawling the floor for his clothes.

Or maybe it wasn't weird at all, and he was just being an insecure idiot!

She was probably outside on the terrace, taking in the morning. She had probably slipped out so as not to wake him, so as not deprive him of rest after last night.

He felt his lips twitching with a smile. An energetic night, to say the least.

Beyond sublime…

He pulled on his jeans.

Bodies entwined, skin to skin, coming undone together over and over again. And no, it wasn't remotely the long game, and no, he hadn't meant for it to happen, but somehow it had.

He gathered his hair up into its tie.

He wasn't sorry, though. How could he be sorry about *that* depth of tenderness, *that* depth of connection? Or about how perfectly they had fit together, flowed together? Her eyes, hazel-soft on his as he had loved her, baring her soul, it felt like. Her touch, so loving. Her kiss, full of everything. How could he be sorry when it had felt so *meant*, and had meant so much? Every breath. Every beat. When suddenly it had felt like he was home, like he was looking at his whole future…

Close to overwhelming. That realisation. The sudden, anchoring certainty of it, the rush of feeling that came with it.

He picked up his top, readying it in his hands. So, no, he wasn't sorry, had no regrets. Only this love beating inside him, beating so hard for her that he hadn't been able to hold it in.

Not that she had heard him say it. She had been sleeping, her breathing soft and rhythmic when he had whispered it into the darkness. But it had felt so good, saying those three words, feeling the shape of them on his lips where her lips had just been. He had wanted to say it to her face this morning, pull her close, kiss her and say it, watch the words land, but now…

He yanked the top on over his head to see off a sigh. Not ideal, waking up alone after a night like that. His heart dipped low. Not what he had expected at all, not after the love they had shared, made, not after all that magic…

Oh God! And now here were the anxious jitters starting up again. Which meant he needed to get out there fast, set his eyes on her lovely face, see her smile, feel the reassurance in it, so he could trust that they were all right.

He headed out the door, pausing in the hallway to listen, but the villa was determinedly silent.

Terrace?

He turned, pushing through the doors into the warm, bright sunshine.

Remnants of last night's dinner on the table. Lounger cushions askew. Empty wine bottle on its side, glinting green against the pale stone.

Their glasses set down, blushing pink with red wine dregs. But no Izzy.

No sight. No sound.

He felt a knot forming in his chest, panic thrumming around it.

Something was off. Definitely. But what?

His heart pulsed. Had he done something wrong? Another pulse. Surely nothing so heinous as to deserve this…this…abandonment… this total absence of her!

Wait…

He went back inside for his phone.

No message!

Had she taken hers? If so, he could call her.

He scouted round. Not in the kitchen. Not in the bedroom with her bag. Not in the sitting room… *There!* By the French doors, still plugged into the outdoor speakers.

He felt his stomach churn and went back outside to draw in a lungful of air. Leaving her phone was the ultimate brush-off. Clearly Izzy did not want to be reached.

A pang seized his chest. Why, though? Why would she do this to him after loving him like that last night? He ground his jaw. *Why? Why? Why?* It simply didn't make—

His breath checked. Or maybe it did fit, did make sense.

He went over to the loungers, straightened

the cushions and sat down. What had she said yesterday as she had been tearing off down the path?

'*You start to question everything, and everyone, but mostly you question yourself...*'

He bit into his lip. Was that what was happening here? Had Izzy taken off to take herself apart, to question herself about last night? To pick holes in it perhaps, in herself, in him?

Hells bells!

And here he was, so high on love, so past the point of no return that it hadn't even occurred to him she might start having second thoughts. She was entitled to them, of course, but not if they were coming from some fanciful notion that he wasn't for real, that his intentions weren't a hundred percent honourable, that he wasn't in it to win it. And not if they were coming from some newly imagined failing in herself, either. Because she was so good at that, imagining weakness inside her.

He got to his feet. If Izzy was having some kind of meltdown, then he needed to find her, talk her off her ledge, reassure her. But where the hell was she? She hadn't taken her bag or her phone, so that probably ruled out town, or anywhere too far away, which left...

His gaze lighted on the terrace steps.

The beach!

Of course. The obvious place!

He set off, taking the steps at speed, going as fast as his bare feet could go. Whatever was up, whatever it took, he was going to turn this around, because last night he had seen the light in Izzy's eyes, seen his whole future right there in her gaze, and he was *not* letting it slip away from him now.

No way!

Not this time!

CHAPTER NINETEEN

Izzy sat down on the boulder and drew her knees up.

What was she doing? Hiding down here wasn't right. It was immature. Worse! She was hurting Finn, because he was bound to be awake by now, wondering where she was, why she had left…

She closed her eyes. Oh, but what else could she have done? Stayed in bed beside him until he woke up and looked at her with last night in his eyes. *Those whispered words.* Saw them there, felt the weight of them bearing down on her, the weight and the expectation.

I love you.

It was so unbelievably ironic! Everything the teenager inside her had ever dreamed of. *Wanted.* But she wasn't a teenager anymore, and this wasn't a dream. Finn was a grown man now, with a grown man's heart, and never mind that last night had been everything it never had been with Eddie. Never mind that every touch, every kiss, every moment had felt perfect. Never mind that she had felt so much love rising inside her she could barely breathe. Fact was, she couldn't live up to this love of Finn's, should never have courted it, never have kissed him, never have started what she couldn't damn well finish!

Panic, clawing at her chest the second he had uttered the words, his voice husky, thick with emotion. Panic, because she didn't *want* the responsibility of Finn's heart. She didn't want to be holding it in her hands. Her hands weren't safe. And if she had only opened her stupid eyes, read Finn's signs and tells properly, the twinkling way he looked at her, his kindnesses, his attentiveness and protectiveness, seen them for what they were, for where they were heading, she could have drawn back, saved him from falling for her. But she hadn't. She had leant on him instead, trading on his sweet attention, lapping it up because she liked the way he made her feel, liked the way he looked at her, and teased her, put sparks in her belly and tingles in her veins.

In other words, she had been selfish and self-centred, and now she had got Finn on the hook, declaring his love for her in the dark. But it was a love she couldn't handle, a love she was bound to mishandle, because she was a walking disaster, didn't know whether she was Arthur or Martha. And she didn't want to hurt him, couldn't bear the thought of it, even though it was exactly what she was doing right now by being AWOL, which only went to prove the point, demonstrate how much of an utter mess she—

'Izzy!'

Her heart lurched.

Oh Lordy!

And now here he was, coming, flying over the beach in his bare feet, skidding to a stop, panting, his eyes wide and loud. 'Are you okay, Iz?'

She felt tears welling in her chest. Of course, that, asking her *that*. Always that care and concern from him first. Never recrimination, which was what she deserved.

She forced a swallow. 'Yes.'

His brow furrowed. 'So, what's going on? Why are you down here?' Incomprehension in his eyes. Hurt. And then a shadow moved through his gaze. 'Is it me? Did I do something wrong?'

Her heart seized.

As if!

But what to say? How to explain, without hurting him more? If only she could think of something that wasn't the painful truth. But it was all she had…

'No, you didn't do anything wrong, Finn.' She got up to face him, because suddenly sitting didn't feel right. 'It was me. I did.'

'What?' His eyes searched hers. 'What are you talking about? What did you do?'

'I kissed you, Finn, started this whole…' She felt the words drying in her mouth, forced another swallow. 'And I shouldn't have. It was a mistake!'

His gaze drained. 'A mistake? But I…' Shaking his head. 'That's not the impression I got from you last night.' And then he was stepping back, his jaw flexing. 'Can I just check? We *were* in the same bed, right?'

The tears in her chest welled harder. Being sarky now. Nothing she didn't deserve. She had deserted him, after all, and now she was pulling the rug out from under him. If he needed to react…

'Yes, we were, but we shouldn't have been.'

'*Why*, though? Why *this*, all of a sudden?' Then he was stepping close again, catching her hands, folding them into his. 'You're going to have to explain it to me, Iz, because I thought we were on the same page last night. I thought that what we had going on was pretty great.' His gaze opened out, reaching into hers. 'Am I wrong?'

A scalding wave arced up her spine. 'No.' Because how could she deny it? They had both been there, loving each other, *loving* the loving.

'What is it, then?' His hands tightened around hers, his fingers intertwining with hers. 'It was great, but now somehow, you've decided it was a mistake, that it shouldn't have happeened.' He dipped his chin. 'You leave me to wake up alone. You come down here. No note to say where you are.' He shook his head. 'And now, now you're just looking at me, giving me nothing, as if we aren't even friends anymore.'

Her heart swung. Only because she couldn't articulate all these disparate feelings. Loving him. Wanting him. But not the responsibility of his heart. Wanting the lightness but none of the weight, none of the expectation. Wanting to have her cake and to eat it, too.

'Aren't we friends, Iz?' His lips flattened. 'Or have I got that wrong?' His hands dropped hers. 'Have I been some kind of colossal mug here? All this time thinking we're friends, getting to be close, when in fact all you ever wanted was a roll in the hay. Wham-bam, thank you Finn, please sign the book on your way out!'

Her heart spasmed.

'No, Finn! Don't. It's not that!'

His hands gripped her shoulders. 'Then what is it, Izzy? Talk to me, please...' Pleading with his eyes, wet eyes now, making her own eyes well. 'Please. Just talk to me.'

Oh God!

But there was no escaping it now.

'All right, I'll tell you...' She squeezed her

lids shut to help the words come. 'I heard what you said, okay? What you whispered. And it—' How to even put it?

But then Finn was saving her the trouble, relaxing his grip on her shoulders. 'It freaked you out.'

Understanding in his voice, drawing fresh tears up.

'Yes.' She opened her eyes. 'It freaked me out.'

His gaze rippled then settled. 'Is it any use pointing out that you weren't meant to hear it?'

'No. Because I did. It's out there now.'

'Okay.' He set his lips. 'So we should talk about it…' But then his eyes clouded over. 'Assuming there's any point. Because obviously, if you don't feel—'

'I *do* feel…' Because whatever the outcome here, he needed to know that, *needed* to know that he had never been just a roll in the hay. Her heart paused. Maybe if she came completely clean, emptied her whole sorry self out into his hands, he *would* believe it. It was the least she could do. And also the best.

She locked her eyes on his, loading her voice so he would feel every word she was saying. 'I like you, Finn, and I care about you, and I *always* have.'

'Always?' He blinked. 'What does that even mean?'

'It means since school. Since the day Carl first brought you home. You came in, and you glanced at me, and that was it. A crush was born. So you see, there it is. *Not* a roll in the hay. And full disclosure...' Because why not go for broke? '*You* are the whole reason I did that stupid show at school. I didn't want to be in it, but you were, and I wanted to be near you just so I could look at you. That's why I said yes to the other two.'

His eyes flickered and then a smile touched his lips, lighting up his gaze. 'I don't believe it. That's when I first noticed *you*, when I...'

Her heart missed a beat. 'When you what?'

'Hell!' His throat rolled. 'It's when I fell for you, Iz. I liked you at school too, loved to watch you rehearsing.'

She felt her eyes staring into his, her heart thumping hard. Could it be true? And then somehow, they were both speaking at once, their words and voices merging. 'That time in the wings!'

Then Finn leapt in. 'I wanted to say something. But you were Carl's sister. I thought it would wreck things with him, didn't want him to know, so I...'

Pennies dropping fast!

'You ignored me.'

Nodding. 'I'm sorry. And then we all scattered, and you met Eddie, so...'

Her heart squeezed. 'You never got a chance with me. Is that what you're saying?'

He gave a little shrug. 'When I saw you in that bar, Iz—'

She cut in. 'I couldn't *believe* it was you! Couldn't believe how *mad* I still felt at you for—'

'And I wanted to make amends, show you—'

'You did, Finn! You showed me how decent you were, so I couldn't stay mad at you. But I knew that if I saw you again, I'd likely get in a tangle—'

'So you blew me off.'

'Yes! Not because you were cramping my style, but because I was scared of liking you again.' She felt her heart sinking, the euphoria of the last few moments fading. 'Which is exactly what's happened these past few days, and the reason I kissed you last night.' She put her hand on his arm so he would feel some warmth coming through her. 'And you're right. It *was* great. *Beyond* great! But then you said what you said, and what had felt great started to feel too big, like too much.'

'So you bolted.'

Her heart twisted. 'I couldn't face you, Finn. Couldn't face seeing love in your eyes that I can't live up to.'

He frowned. Then his hand lifted to her cheek. 'It's not something you have to live up to, Izzy.

It's not a gold standard or anything. It simply exists, is patient and kind, et cetera. It's nothing to be scared of. I get that you're full of doubts and insecurities because of Eddie. You spent all that time with him when you didn't really love him, but look at us. Just stop and think about *us* for a second…

'Here we are now on this teeny tiny island after how many years, not only on the same island, but in the same bar on the same night at exactly the same moment. We're staying less than a kilometre apart. You're single. I'm single. You've always liked me. I've always liked you…' A smile played over his lips. 'If I didn't know better, I'd almost think the universe was trying to tell us something.'

Her heart stilled.

Compelling…

Almost as compelling as the light in his eyes. Warm amber, lit with love. The dream she had dreamed so long ago. Now it was finally here, real, warming her face, filling her heart. And she was facing it, wasn't she? Looking it in the eye, not feeling scared. But even so…

She covered her hand with his. 'I just don't want to hurt you, Finn, break your heart, because it's such a good heart. And I'm such a mess.'

'Oh, Izzy…' His other hand came up, cupping her face, his gaze soft on hers. 'You've got some difficult stuff to sort out. I know that. But you're *not* a mess, and you need to stop thinking of yourself in that way. You're not going to break my heart, not if you love me.' He was stroking his thumbs over her cheekbones now, setting off a sweet, tingling ache inside her. Then his chin dipped, his eyes soft with hope. 'Do you love me, Izzy?'

Those eyes… That question…

Sharpening her focus somehow, bringing clarity. Sweet, crisp, beautiful, joyous clarity!

This was Finn Falco, the only one she had ever wanted to be with, the one whose name she had scribbled in endless hearts in her secret diary, the one who had played drums with his band in all the school shows, looking so hot in his T-shirt with his nice honed arms. *This* was Finn Falco, the one who had rescued her from her drunken tabletop in that bar. The one who had brought her breakfast and saved her from a leaking ice cream cone. The one who had lifted her up when she was down, had made her laugh with his teasing. The one who made the sky seem bluer and the sun seem brighter. And the one who had made love to her last night like he meant it, like he meant to see her through. *Of course* she loved him! And now she needed to tell him…

She put her hands to his cheeks, feeling the

love inside her rise into her eyes. 'Yes, I love you, Finn.' And how good did it feel to be saying it, setting it free at last? 'I think I've probably loved you forever.'

His eyes lit, then he broke into his beautiful easy-going smile. 'I'll take forever all day long.'

And then he was moving in, kissing her, and his kiss felt warm and tender and perfect, so right that it was almost as if the universe itself had planned it…

EPILOGUE

Six months later...

FINN HUGGED THE WALL, inching toward the doorway until he had eyes on Izzy, sitting cross-legged in the centre of the vast bed, her gaze trained on her laptop screen.

He held his breath, but he couldn't hold back his smile any more than he could stop his heart turning cartwheels. This sight never grew old, especially when Iz was in a singing mood, which she was. He had heard her the second he had entered the hotel suite, singing an old favourite, and any second, she was going to strike up again, which was when he would also strike...

She tapped a key, fingering a stray lock of hair back into place and then her shoulders started to move rhythmically, her head joining in...

'Girls Amok gonna work round the clock, oh yeah, oh yeah...'

Twirling her hands, giving it the cute overbite.

'Girls Amok gonna chock your block, oh yeah, oh yeah, oh yeah...'

He moved himself into launch position.

'Chock your block, yeah, yeah.' Pointing ahead now. 'Cos we got the power to turn sweet sour, shower your hour with—'

He sprang, throwing out a pointing hand. 'Whole meal flour, oh yeah—'

Izzy jolted, clutching at her chest, and then she turned the death ray on him. 'Oh-my-God-Finn-will-you-*stop*-doing that! You scared the living daylights out me.'

Too funny!

'Sorry. Couldn't resist.'

She twisted her mouth to the side, but in the next moment, she was smiling. 'You can never resist.'

His heart filled. 'I can never resist *you*.'

Her eyes fired him a warning. 'I'm working.'

His heart filled again, with pride this time. Working for herself now and doing well. Her own graphic design business. Autonomy at last. And, helpfully, a business she could run from anywhere, which mostly—*happily*—meant from whichever hotel or rental place he was staying in.

He felt an inside smile unwinding. Who knew that they could have become so inseparable so quickly? But those last few days in Croatia, before she had gone back home to extricate herself from Eddie, had set them up. Ironically, it had felt like a honeymoon. Riding round the island on his bike, swimming, walking. Lots of talking. He had even got to take her to that swanky beach club for lunch, the place with the private al fresco tables and billowing white curtains…

They had packed so much into those few days. So much living. So much laughter. So much love and loving. Izzy had given up on her doubts, had embraced the circularity idea, that they had ended up where they were meant to be all along. He didn't doubt it for a second, which was why he had a little something tucked up his sleeve for her, or rather, in the back pocket of his jeans…

He went to stretch out on the bed beside her, picking up the thread he had left hanging. 'Sounded more like singing than working.'

Her eyes glanced into his. 'It helps me to concentrate.'

'What? All those great lyrics!'

She giggled. 'I know. Utter pants. But see, poor Girls Amok don't have a Jaxon Cairns to hand. As for your "whole meal flour"…' Her gaze slid to his. 'Just don't give up the day job, is all I'm saying.'

He clapped his hand to his chest to tease her. 'You don't like my lyric? I'm devastated.'

She turned, offering up a smile, and then she was closing her laptop and lying down, snuggling into him. 'Don't be devastated. You're a very good drummer.' Caressing his chest. 'You're very good at a lot of things…'

He felt a smile coming, alongside the usual stirring below decks. 'I thought you were working.'

'I'm taking a break.' And then her palm flattened against his chest. 'So, how was the video shoot?'

'Quite similar to the last one. Lots of waiting around, lots of walking backwards and forwards in front of a green screen. We got water poured all over us this time, though, so, you know…'

'Wet.'

'Yep, and cold!'

But he didn't want to be talking about the video, not when he had a more pressing agenda.

He looked at the ceiling to see off a flutter of nerves. Was this the right moment, though? Mid-afternoon on a workday. Should he have been going a bit more to town, doing this in a grander style at some hashtag-oh-so-romantic location?

Earlier he had decided not, since marriage might well still be a touchy subject for Izzy. He didn't want to scare her. He wanted the opposite. To show her where he stood. Quietly. Gently. He wanted her to know he was in this for the duration. And so…

He shifted, turning toward her. 'Iz, are you happy?'

Her eyes looked into each of his in turn, as if she was expecting a tease. Then her gaze cleared, filling with a smile. 'Yes, Finn. I'm very, very happy.'

Music to his ears, and to his heart!

He touched her face. 'So, how about we make this official?'

Her eyes flitted to each of his in turn again, and then her lips curved up a little. 'Are you asking me what I think you're asking me?'

'I don't know. If it involves a ring, then yes, that's the question I'm asking.'

Her lips pressed together. 'So ask it, then. Properly.'

His heart smiled.

Izzy...

'You want me to do the knee thing?'

She shook her head. 'No, right here is perfect. But you have to ask.'

'Okay.' He pulled out the box and popped the lid. Then he looked into her eyes, seeing heaven, as always. 'Izzy Valentine, will you marry me?'

She held his gaze, on and on, giving his heart conniptions, until suddenly her face broke apart and she was smiling again, her eyes glistening, beaming light and love and the rest of his life right back at him.

'Yes, Finn Falco. I will. And let's do it soon, because I *can't wait* to marry you!'

* * * * *

If you enjoyed this story, check out these other great reads from Ella Hayes.

**Driving Her Impossible Billionaire
Bound by Their Lisbon Legacy
One Night on the French Riviera
Barcelona Fling with a Secret Prince**

All available now!

Get up to 4 Free Books!

We'll send you 2 free books from each series you try
PLUS a free Mystery Gift.

Both the **Harlequin® Historical** and **Harlequin® Romance** series feature compelling novels filled with emotion and simmering romance.

YES! Please send me 2 FREE novels from the Harlequin Historical or Harlequin Romance series and my FREE Mystery Gift (gift is worth about $10 retail). I may cancel anytime by emailing ReaderServiceInfo@Harlequin.com or by calling 1-800-873-8635. If I don't cancel, I will receive 5 new Harlequin Historical books every month and be billed just $6.39 each in the U.S. or $7.19 each in Canada, or 4 new Harlequin Romance Larger-Print books every month and be billed just $7.19 each in the U.S. or $7.99 each in Canada, a savings of 20% off the cover price. It's quite a bargain! Shipping and handling is just 75¢ per book in the U.S. and $1.75 per book in Canada.* I understand that accepting the free books and gift places me under no obligation to buy anything—they are mine to keep for free no matter what I decide.

Choose one:
- ☐ Harlequin Historical (246/349 BPA G3CD)
- ☐ Harlequin Romance Larger-Print (119/319 BPA G3CD)
- ☐ Or Try Both! (246/349 & 119/319 BPA G3CE)

Name (please print)

Address   Apt. #

City   State/Province   Zip/Postal Code

Email: Please check this box ☐ if you would like to receive newsletters and promotional emails from Harlequin Enterprises ULC and its affiliates. You can unsubscribe anytime.

Mail to the **Harlequin Reader Service:**
IN U.S.A.: P.O. Box 1341, Buffalo, NY 14240-8531
IN CANADA: P.O. Box 603, Fort Erie, Ontario L2A 5X3

Want to explore our other series or interested in ebooks? Visit www.ReaderService.com or call 1-800-873-8635.

*Terms and prices subject to change without notice. Prices do not include sales taxes, which will be charged (if applicable) based on your state or country of residence. Canadian residents will be charged applicable taxes. Offer not valid in Quebec. This offer is limited to one order per household. Books received may not be as shown. Not valid for current subscribers to the Harlequin Historical or Harlequin Romance series. All orders subject to approval. Credit or debit balances in a customer's account(s) may be offset by any other outstanding balance owed by or to the customer. Please allow 4 to 6 weeks for delivery. Offer available while quantities last.

Your Privacy — Your information is being collected by Harlequin Enterprises ULC, operating as Harlequin Reader Service. For a complete summary of the information we collect, how we use this information and to whom it is disclosed, please visit our privacy notice located at https://corporate.harlequin.com/privacy-notice. Notice to California Residents—Under California law, you have specific rights to control and access your data. For more information on these rights and how to exercise them, visit https://corporate.harlequin.com/california-privacy. For additional information for residents of other U.S. states that provide their residents with certain rights with respect to personal data, visit https://corporate.harlequin.com/other-state-residents-privacy-rights.

HHHRLP2603